Harlequin Romances

OTHER
Harlequin Romances
by MARY BURCHELL

Honey

by

MARY BURCHELL

Harlequin Books

TORONTO • LONDON • NEW YORK • AMSTERDAM • SYDNEY • WINNIPEG

Original hardcover edition published in 1959
by Mills & Boon Limited

ISBN 0-373-02061-9

Harlequin edition published April 1977

Printed in U.S.A.

CHAPTER ONE

EVERYONE called her Honey, though she had been christened—with some forethought—Enid Frederica. Enid after her mother and Frederica after her rich Great-uncle Fred, who was cast for the role of godfather by Mrs. Milward in a moment of maternal optimism not afterwards justified. For when Great-uncle Fred was eventually gathered to his fathers he meanly left his godchild no more than a Toby jug and two hideous oil paintings of doubtful authenticity, while a rather obscure charity, benefited to the tune of something like 20,000 pounds.

But though Honey was faintly chagrined when Great-uncle Fred gave her this posthumous brush-off, she was not one to mourn unduly about things she couldn't do anything about.

"We were never meant to be rich, I guess," she said equably to her mother. "Let the old gentleman rest in peace."

Mrs. Milward, normally the kindest of women, said nevertheless that this was letting Great-uncle Fred off too lightly. But her husband, a busy lawyer in Forchester, the nearest big town, remarked with rather maddening professional acumen, "Well, well, that's the way with most wills. Nobody's ever satisfied. You'd be surprised how often disgruntled relatives unburden themselves to me."

"I wouldn't describe myself as a disgruntled relative," said Mrs. Milward, bridling over the justness of her cause.

"Nor would any of the others," replied her husband good-humoredly.

"Well, I'm glad we never really called Honey Frederica, anyway," Mrs. Milward retorted.

"So am I," Honey said, laughing.

It was her adored older brother, Michael, who had first given her the name. For when some well-meaning visitor had gushed over the new baby and said, "Isn't she *sweet!*" Michael, from the superior height of five years, had surveyed the golden fluff on her head and said, "She ought to be. She's got honey on top."

The hair had darkened a little throughout the years, but the silly name had stuck. Perhaps because she really was a honey, or perhaps because in summer her smooth skin tanned to honey gold color. At any rate, there was something appropriate about the name, and Honey she had remained.

The Milwards lived in a big, pleasant, slightly shabby but indefinably elegant house on the outskirts of Meadlands, the prettiest village in the whole county of Edomshire. Every day Mr. Milward drove the 20-odd miles into Forchester, and once a week his wife accompanied him to do her shopping.

Michael, having grown up into quite a brilliant building engineer, had gone off some years ago to build bridges in remote parts of the world. But, even now, he was apt to turn up without warning from the ends of the earth and arrive on the parental doorstep, secure in the knowledge that his sister would welcome him with hugs and kisses, his mother with a few tears, and his father with a great show of having expected him anyway. All of which meant, of course, that they were enchanted to see him.

The last time he had done this, Honey had not been available to play her part with her usual fervor, for she had been in the throes of her first few months' of training at St. Margaret's, the big general hospital in Forchester. And, although she was lucky to be sufficiently near home to rush there on her free days, no one who has gone through those first few gruelling months in a big hospital will be surprised to hear that, once she was off duty, Honey's one idea had been to get off her aching feet and relax.

But those days were far behind her now. Honey had entered her third year at St. Margaret's and had an air of calm efficiency that proved itself against most emergencies. Though not all, she thought, as she stood at the dining-room window looking over the early summertime beauty of the garden—not all. Not, for instance, that unlucky brush with Dr. Anston.

Honey was just starting on a week's vacation and had meant to celebrate the first day by having breakfast in bed. But habit and the soft June sunshine had been too much for her, and so here she was—downstairs before her parents, idling away the few minutes before breakfast and trying not to think of Dr. Anston.

Most people were a little afraid of the brilliant plastic surgeon, who came from London once—and sometimes twice—a week to operate at St. Margaret's. Only the patients saw no fault in him, overlooking everything but the fact that those strong, fine, beautiful hands could restore them to normal happy life when they had desperately feared that they must go on through the years disfigured or deformed.

At one time Honey had not feared him either, because she too thought that genius was entitled to indulge in curtness and some sarcasm which need not be taken too much to heart. But recently there had been a series of unfortunate happenings—beginning with the time when she had impulsively and inexplicably spoken up in defense of a petrified nurse who had incurred his wrath.

It was one of those occasions when one, if wise, held one's peace, however much one might seethe inside. But Honey had rushed indignantly to the defense of the other girl. If she had stopped short of saying that the great man was being unjust, she had somehow managed to imply that she thought he was.

Sister's eyes had almost popped out of her head, and afterward Honey had received a severe reprimand. But Sister's sharp words were dew and rose petals compared to the awful experience of having Dr. Anston fix his glance upon her for long seconds in a sort of reflective chilliness. Then, when her temperature was well below normal, he said, "It's good of you, Nurse, to let us have your valuable and refreshing views. But you are troubling yourself unduly. I am capable of assessing a situation myself." That was all. ("And enough, too" as Barbara Conway, Honey's special friend at St. Margaret's, afterward remarked.) But Honey was on duty in Dr. Anston's operating room, and so she saw him week after week. He never addressed her personally again. But occasionally, between cases, his coolly reflective gray eyes would regard her over his mask, and she would know that he recognized her as the nurse who had not known her place.

All this would have been bad enough. But only a

few days before she had gone on vacation—recently enough to spoil one's holiday if one did not stop thinking about the incident—Honey, coming off duty, had paused in the narrow pathway between the hospital and the nurses' residence to have a word with Barbara and a second-year nurse called Manners.

Manners was declaring that Dr. Edwards, one of the visiting physicians, was the most exacting creature on earth, but Honey felt that this assertion must be challenged. Forgetting the foolishness of expressing criticism near the hospital premises, she said clearly and feelingly, "Oh, but, my dear, just thank God on your knees that you don't work for Dr. Anston. He may be handsome and he may be a genius, but if you cross him he's a monster. Why, he—"

She stopped, because suddenly she realized that Barbara's countenance had become a queer, greenish shade, while Manners was opening and shutting her mouth wordlessly, like a goldfish. Then a familiar voice said, almost at her elbow, "Good evening, Nurse," and Dr. Anston passed, leaving behind him a silence as profound as if he had donned the black cap and delivered fatal judgment.

"Do you think he heard?" asked Honey in a whisper when he had passed far beyond shouting range.

Barbara tried gallantly to insist that she thought not. But her companion was depressingly realistic.

"He couldn't have failed to," she said glumly. Then there seemed little else to say. So they had gone their separate ways, the other two girls taking leave of Honey much as prisoners in the French Revolution must have done when the selection for the tumbrils had been announced. . . .

Oh well—Honey gave a resigned shrug and turned

5

away from the window as her mother entered the room. The thought of Dr. Anston was not going to spoil her week's holiday.

"Hello, darling." Her mother's air was affectionate but preoccupied. "You're coming to the meeting this afternoon, aren't you?"

"The meeting?" Honey smiled inquiringly, knowing that her mother discharged with enthusiasm and efficiency a number of public duties.

"It's our group meeting—the Women's Institute, you know. And Madame Seroni is going to speak for us. Such a triumph to get such an interesting and unusual speaker." And Mrs. Milward, from whom Honey had inherited her lovely smile, looked as pleased as a child who unexpectedly finds itself at the top of the class.

"Your capture, I take it?" Honey looked amused but respectful.

"Yes." It was obvious from Mrs. Milward's serene air that the simple, triumphant affirmative needed no embellishing.

"But I thought she was a singer, not a speaker."

"She is a singer, darling. A very famous singer. Command performances of 'Messiah' and that sort of thing. She must have lots of the most enchanting reminiscences and, although she is getting on now, I believe she is still very handsome, which does help. Particularly at a group meeting," added Mrs. Milward, whose meaning will be clear to all who have suffered from the type of lecturer who should be heard and not seen.

"She moved quite recently into the neighbourhood, didn't she?" said Honey, coming to the table.

"Oh, yes! Or else there wouldn't have been a hope

of getting her. Not a hope," declared Mrs. Milward, also sitting down and beginning to flip through her mail, but with a casual air that showed she meant to complete the story of her prize capture. "Mrs. Turtle was the Convener this year, so of course the speaker was really her affair. But, though I don't want to be unkind, she has no inspiration above talks on bee-keeping or the travels of some dull writer or other. And then I heard about Madame Seroni coming to the neighborhood, and like a flash—but really like a flash—the idea came to me: Why not ask her for the group meeting? So with Mrs. Turtle's agreement, I wrote—because it's a little more impressive, you know, dear, if the chairman writes—and her accept-ance came by return mail."

"I daresay she was gratified to be asked," said Honey with a smile. "I'll certainly come to the meet-ing and witness your triumph."

Mrs. Milward smiled modestly in her turn and helped herself to coffee.

"I hope I'm not un-christianlike," she said, obvi-ously fearing that she was, "but when I told Miss Emms, I knew exactly what the Bible means by being puffed up with pride. Because she will sit in the front row and look as though I don't know anything, just because she was a founder member of the Institute 18 years ago. But when I told her the news about Mad-ame Seroni, Miss Emms hadn't a word to say. Not one word."

"Impossible," said Honey's father, coming in and dropping a kiss on his wife's smooth cheek. "I've known Selina Emms for 40 years, and in all that time she's never changed the shape of her hats nor been at a loss for words. Hello, Honey. Good to be home and free from worries?" He bent and kissed her on the cheek.

Honey thought of Dr. Anston. But she smiled at her father and said, "Very good." Then she poured out his coffee for him while her mother attended to her letters. She was just about to ask about Michael's most recent news, when a slight cry from Mrs. Milward drew the attention of both of them.

"Oh, no! No, that's impossible! She can't do that." Honey's mother began to scrabble distractedly through the rest of her letters, as though she might find something to contradict whatever had overwhelmed her in the first one.

"What is it?" Honey looked half-frightened.

"It's . . . it's Madame Seroni." Her mother choked on something suspiciously like a sob. "She says she can't come, after all. That she's going to London today. Just like that. As this were any day."

"But she can't!" Honey caught the infection of her mother's near panic. "She promised."

"Who," inquired Mr. Milward, with ill-judged mildness, "is Madame Seroni?"

"I told you!" his wife cried reproachfully. "She's our speaker for the group meeting. And now she says she can't come."

"Well, these things do happen," Mr. Milward said, with the incredible philosophy of one not personally involved. "You'll just have to get someone else. I suppose there are other speakers."

"The meeting," stated Mrs. Milward, looking at her husband as though she wondered for the first time why she had married him, "is this afternoon. And Miss Emms will be sitting in the front row, waiting for something to go wrong. And all the other brilliantly efficient chairmen of all the other institutes in the group will be there on the platform. And the secretaries too, if there's room," she added, in distracted parenthesis. "And the county representative. And there's *no speaker.*"

"Honey will speak to them on nursing," suggested Mr. Milward with unwelcome humor.

"They don't *want* Honey." Mrs. Milward, who very properly thought her child the best and most wonderful child on earth, dismissed Honey on this occasion with a flick of her hand. "They've been promised a celebrity and they expect a celebrity."

"Can't you just apologize and say—"

"Oh, don't be *stupid!*" cried poor Mrs. Milward. "You can't apologize to 217 women who are expecting to be entertained."

"It's a formidable thought," her husband conceded.

"If I didn't think they'd be bored to tears, I'd make you come along and talk to them about law," said Mrs. Milward, frankness getting the better of her natural politeness.

"And if I had time," replied her husband, somewhat piqued by this, "I'd come and prove to you all that law can be absorbing. But I haven't time," he added hastily and getting to his feet, he saw a fanatical gleam come into his wife's eye. "I must go now."

"But this afternoon, James—"

"Quite impossible, darling. Case of Jones v. Jones," declared her husband firmly. "Goodby—" He kissed his wife and patted Honey's head as he passed. "Don't worry. It will turn out all right in the end."

And off he went to what he mistakenly supposed were more pressing problems.

"And then they say, Honey, that your father's an exceptionally intelligent man," Mrs. Milward said, looking after him. Turn out all right in the end, indeed! With Miss Emms in the front row and no speaker!"

Honey, truly sorry for her mother and realizing the depth of her humiliating predicament, made one or two tentative suggestions for a substitute speaker. But Mrs. Milward dismissed the vicar as lacking in novelty value and Miss Cutts, the local literary light, with the simple but devastating statement, "She will read her own poetry."

"Then I suggest we make one more bid for Madame Seroni," Honey declared, studying the letter that her mother had passed to her. "She says she is going to London today. I don't see how she can go before the 11:30 train. Suppose I cycle over and explain to her. That's much more telling than a phone call. And she probably doesn't even realize what a crisis she's precipitated."

"Oh, Honey! Would you really, darling? I've so much else to do for the meeting, and if anyone could persuade her, you could. Don't you mind tackling her?"

"Not in the least," said Honey, thinking of Dr. Anston and restraining herself with difficulty from saying that her mother lived a more sheltered life than she realized.

"You know the house, don't you?" Mrs. Milward followed her daughter out into the hall. "The one with the whitewashed walls and the green shutters—just about three miles out on the road to Forchester. It's called Four Trees, but the name was worn off the gate long ago, and there are only three trees now.

But, of course, the name hasn't been changed."

"I know." Honey was reassuring. "Old Mrs. Aitken lived there for about 100 years. Do you think I look presentable enough to interview a prima donna? Or shall I try to look more fetching?" She critically studied her reflection in the hall mirror.

"You look lovely, darling," declared her mother. "That green linen is just right with your fair hair." And she too looked in the mirror for a moment and thought that Madame Seroni would have to be hard-hearted indeed to resist the appeal of Honey's big brown eyes and her soft, smiling red mouth. "Don't you want a jacket?"

"No. It will be warm cycling. Try not to worry," Honey said kindly, as she wheeled her bicycle onto the gravel drive. "I'll bring back an acceptance from Madame Seroni, or perish in the attempt."

"Oh no, dear. Not that," amended Mrs. Milward, seeing things in better proportion for a moment. But Honey only laughed and, mounting her bicycle, waved and set off.

It was wonderful gliding smoothly along the road in the sunshine, with no one to remind her of 101 duties or an almost stop-watch routine. The birds sang and the warm, sweet scent of the clover drifted to her from the nearby fields. A few clouds rode high in the sky, and occasionally a cloud-shadow passed slowly over the landscape. Everything seemed so peaceful and radiant that Honey knew she was going to make a success of her mission. Her qualms were so few that she hardly even rehearsed her opening sentences.

As the road was a good one, she made excellent time, and long before Madame Seroni could be thinking of leaving for the 11:30 train, Honey was cycling up the long drive to the imposing Four Trees.

Dismounting, she propped her bicycle against the side of the porch and rang the bell. Almost immediately she heard the sound of footsteps crossing the hall. The door was opened by an elderly maid of somewhat forbidding appearance.

"I wonder if I might see Madame Seroni." Honey smiled in her most winning manner. "It's rather urgent or I wouldn't—"

"I'm sorry. Madame is away. She went to London this morning."

"She's gone?" Honey was aghast, because somehow she had allowed her natural optimism to override possibilities. "But she can't have gone. The 11:30 is the first train."

"Madame travels by car," replied the maid with superb contempt for any other form of locomotion. "She will be back tomorrow night."

She was away for only two days, and one of them had to be the day of the group meeting!

"Tomorrow night will be too late," Honey said, and even to her own ears that sounded rather excessively tragic. The maid actually looked slightly disturbed and started to say something else. But at that moment a second person crossed the hall and Honey, who thought that she must have wandered into a nightmare, heard an unmistakable voice say, "What is it, Palmer?"

"It's a young lady wanting Madame, sir." The maid spoke over her shoulder. "But I've just been explaining that she's already gone."

Then Palmer stepped aside to disclose to Honey's incredulous and horrified gaze Dr. Anston, looking very much at ease in gray flannel slacks and white shirt. She was completely taken aback by him.

"I'm afraid—" he began. Then he stopped. "Good morning, Nurse." The tone had changed subtly. "What are you doing in this part of the world?"

"I . . . live here," explained Honey, with a confused belief that she had no right to be living anywhere at the moment.

"Do you really? Won't you come in and let met see if I can do anything for you?"

If she had retained any common sense, of course, Honey would have said there was nothing he could do and fled from the spot. But Palmer was already opening the door wide to disclose a beautiful square, panelled hall. Fascinated, Honey entered the house, which Dr. Anston seemed so unaccountably to be at home in.

"I gather it was my aunt you wanted, but—"

"Your *aunt?*" Honey was shocked into exclaiming, for somehow one does not think of the Olympians as having aunts. "Is Madame Seroni your aunt?"

"Yes. Even monsters have relatives, you know," he replied carelessly. So carelessly that it was a moment before Honey realized what he had said. Then the implication hit her with the shock of delayed action, so that she blushed furiously and dropped her eyes.

Was it something quite personal, or can I help?" Dr. Anston sounded studiously polite, but she had the curious impression that he was enjoying himself.

"It . . . it was about the group meeting," stammered Honey, demoralized by the reference to monsters but clinging gallantly to the purpose of her visit. "The group meeting of the Women's Institutes. Your...I mean Madame Seroni was to be the speaker. And now she's gone away and the meeting is this afternoon.

There are I don't know how many women coming, expecting a brilliant and entertaining speaker. My mother, who is a darling and the chairman responsible for everything going smoothly, is at her wits' end. I thought if I came over and explained to Madame Seroni, she might understand and cancel her London visit. But she's gone already, so I don't know *what* we can do."

"I see." Dr. Anston looked so gravely reflective that Honey immediately suspected him of laughing at her. For she could not imagine that a busy and famous surgeon would really concern himself with the details of a village crisis.

"I don't expect you see at all," she was rather frightened to hear herself say. But she was goaded on by a sort of angry protectiveness toward her mother and all the other kind, ordinary people whose affairs were deeply important to themselves, even if despised by Dr. Anston. "I suppose you think a Women's Institute is a rather comic sort of gathering where a lot of women talk a good deal and do nothing, and that even if my mother is humiliated by failing her friends, it's all very trivial and—"

"Just a moment." Dr. Anston raised his hand, in the gesture that was reputed to quell the most unruly class of students in a matter of seconds. It reduced Honey to instantaneous silence.

"It would be better," he said drly, "if you would let me speak for myself instead of saddling me with views I don't hold in order to berate me for my wrong-headed notions. To begin with, I happen to know quite a lot about Women's Institutes—"

"Do you?" gasped Honey, pleasurably shocked by the incongruity of this.

"—and there is not very much," he went on, "that you can tell me about the solid work and the goodness of heart to be found among their members. When I was a young doctor, just beginning—" Honey gasped again because somehow one never thought of Dr. Anston as anything but supremely confident and successful. I worked in a scattered rural district. I had plenty of occasion to bless the Institute's friendliness and efficiency. And because of those days and not at all because you have seen fit to lecture me on my natural callousness of disposition, I will very willingly help your mother out of this fix, if I can. How would it do if I gave them a talk?"

"*You*, Dr. Anston!" Honey was filled with astonishment and remorse, but a certain amount of misgiving crept in. "It's . . . it's awfully good of you, and I think —" once more she hastily reviewed and rejected, the vicar and the local poetess "—I think my mother would be tremendously grateful."

"Very well."

"But—" Honey had a vision of Dr. Anston lecturing the group meeting in the cool, precise and academic terms of a medical school "—they like something very *human* you know."

"Meaning that I am inhuman?"

"Oh no!" Honey blushed to the roots of her hair, aware that the truth had crept out. "I . . . I didn't mean anything personal. I meant the type of talk, you know. *That's* what has to be human. Nothing about anatomy or anything like that," she concluded feebly.

"I'll do my best," said Dr. Anston gravely. "Where is the meeting?"

"At the Village Hall in Meadlands—at two-thirty."

"Very well. Tell your mother I'll be there."

With the confused impression that she was presenting the group meeting with either a triumphant success or a disastrous failure. Honey groped once more for a suitable expression of gratitude.

"It's extraordinarily kind of you," she said shyly.

"Not at all." The doctor's smile was faintly sardonic but not without charm. "I feel there is a sort of family responsibility involved. It was really too bad of my aunt to let your mother down in this way. But she is an artist and inclined to think her own affairs rank above any others. I am sure she had no idea of the crisis she was precipitating."

"Well, it's quite all right now." Honey said, hoping profoundly that it was. Then there seemed nothing to do but to take leave of him.

Dr. Anston accompanied her to the door, Honey feeling all the time that she really, ought to say something in the way of apology—both for the manner in which she had lectured the most distinguished surgeon at St. Margaret's, and for the most unfortunate term she had used to describe him in the conversation he had all too obviously overheard. But it was difficult to think of anything casual or graceful when he looked so unfairly cool and remote, and she felt so shaken and gauche.

He watched her mount her bicycle, and even this she did with less than her usual skill because Dr. Anston was looking on. Then he raised his hand in an amused gesture of something more like dismissal than farewell. And Honey, her errand completed, rode off down the drive once more.

All the way home she was reliving the incredible encounter and thinking of the cool, dignified, and telling things she might have said. But, alas, all that was too late now. Her rash and indignant indictment could only have confirmed his obvious belief that she was both foolish and rude.

Depressed as she was over these reflections and by the general feeling of failure, Honey was both astonished and pleased to receive unstinted praise from her mother on the new arrangement.

"Why, Honey darling, how resourceful of you! What a wonderful way to save the day. And how incredibly fortunate that he happened to be a friend of yours."

Honey winced. "Not exactly a friend," she murmured feelingly.

"Well, I know, of course, that there is a professional and social gap between a famous surgeon and a third year nurse," Mrs. Milward conceded cheerfully. She obviously thought that when a nurse was as pretty as her own Honey, the gap insensibly narrowed. "But I'm sure he wouldn't have done it for just anybody. However kind he may be," she added, enthusiastic for the beauty of her rescuer's disposition.

Honey wanted to say that Dr. Anston was not at all kind and that her mother was gathering a very curious and idealized impression of him. But, with so many problems still to attend to, it seemed a shame at any rate to shatter her mother's peace of mind on the important topic of the speaker.

"I only hope he won't be too academic," was all she said.

"Oh, I'm sure he won't! And there's something so romantic about a famous surgeon. And a plastic surgeon at that. Think of the human stories he must have among his reminiscences. Is he anything to look at?"

Honey was silent for a moment, trying to consider

the question of Dr. Anston's looks objectively.

"I suppose," she said reluctantly at last, "most people would call him very good-looking. He's tall, medium fair, and has tremendously intelligent, rather cold gray eyes."

"Splendid!" said Mrs. Milward absently, as she wrote out price tickets for the market stall. "He sounds exactly what we want."

"Oh, Mother, don't be sentimental," cried Honey crossly. Her mother merely smiled and said, "But I am sentimental, darling. Most nice, middle-aged women are. How old is your Dr. Anston and what is his other name?"

"Oh, I suppose he's in his mid-thirties and no one ever calls him by his other name, I'm sure," Honey declared.

"They must, dear. His mother couldn't have called him Dr. Anston when he was in knee-pants," declared Mrs. Milward, thereby conjuring up such an unusual view of the man that Honey was struck dumb for a moment.

Then she said meekly, "I know his initials are J.O. I suppose he's John or James or something."

"I shall ask him" replied Mrs. Milward, still writing price tickets.

"Mother, you can't!" All Honey's professional instincts were outraged. "One isn't on those terms with the consultants."

"What terms? I will be the chairman," replied Mrs. Milward, with an air of sweet obstinacy. "And I will say, 'What is your full name, Dr. Anston, as I have to announce you. What would you like me to say about you?' "

Honey gave up then, because if Mother *would* not

understand about Dr. Anston, she would just have to accept the snub when it occurred. The rest of the morning resolved itself into a sort of ordered rush, involving half a dozen trips to the charming village hall a mild discussion on decorations, a very passionate one about who was to sit where on the platform, and a considerable exchange of congratulation on the admirable refreshments that were fast being assembled under the experienced management of Mrs. Turtle.

"It all looks very nice." Mrs. Milward drew a sigh of relief as she stood beside Honey taking a final view of the hall before hurrying home to a brief lunch. "I do hope it's going to be a success."

"I'm sure it will be," Honey declared positively. The more positively as the shadow of Miss Emms's hat fell across them. "Miss Emm's authoritative and mannish voice said, "I still think, Enid—" she always addressed Mrs. Milward as though she were a school prefect "—that it would have been wiser to use teapots instead of the urn. Urn tea never tastes the same."

"But for rapid serving the urn is almost essential," insisted Mrs. Milward. "Nothing's worse than having half of your visitors enjoying their tea while the others sit with their tongues hanging out, waiting for kettles to boil."

Miss Emms smiled pityingly. "It's a question of organization," she said. "I remember just before the war, when I happened to be chairman, there was a giant rally at Duneldon. We served 500 teas in something like a quarter of an hour—all from teapots."

Mrs. Milward smiled politely, while obviously struggling with one word, "Liar!"

"But of course those were other days," added Miss

Emms—a generalization that cannot be denied but can carry the most insulting implications. "I do hope you were right in getting this singing woman to come. I'm not very happy about it."

"Oh, but haven't you heard?" Mrs. Milward's face lit up with pleasure and pride. "Madame Seroni can't come after all, but we have been most fortunate in securing the very distinguished services of the famous plastic surgeon, Dr. Anston." She was obviously releasing her opening remarks.

"Did that change go before the committee for approval?" inquired Miss Emms, undefeated.

"No, of course not. The change was only made this morning," countered Mrs. Milward.

Up went Miss Emms's scanty eyebrows and she jammed her hat farther down on her head.

"Then you mean, Enid, that no one knows anything about this man?"

"Of course they do!" cried Mrs. Milward lightheart-edly. "He's a great friend of Honey's—"

"Oh, Mother!"

"—And generally considered the most brilliant sur-geon at St. Margaret's," continued Mrs. Milward, undeterred. "We were extraordinarily lucky to get him. I believe he is a very handsome man with a fund of human anecdotes, both amusing and moving."

Even Miss Emms looked impressed by this and only recovered sufficiently to say it was a pity it was not a woman surgeon, before Mrs. Milward and Honey said firm goodbyes and left the hall.

"Tiresome woman," exclaimed Mrs. Milward, as they walked down the village street together; but it was evident that she was not really ruffled, for she was secure in the firm conviction that all she had said was true. She's much too finicky about everything, she is."

Lunch was a hurried affair, and almost before it was over, buses, carrying their quota of Institute members from other villages, were speeding past the house on their way to the village hall. One or two ladies of the committee called in as they were about to leave their house, and one of them said to Honey, "I'm so glad your friend was able to come, Honey. It would have been dreadful if there had been no speaker."

"Dr. Anston isn't exactly a friend," Honey began.

"No, no, of course not. I know. But your knowing him made all the difference."

Honey thought of Dr. Anston's nasty speech about rejecting her lecture on his general callousness.

"I don't think I really had much to do with it," she said modestly. But this disclaimer was brushed aside with a laugh, and Honey gave up the impossible task of explaining her exact relationship with Dr. Anston.

When they arrived at the hall her mother said, "You'd better wait at the door and make him welcome. After all, you're the only person who will recognize him."

"As he's the only man attending the meeting, that shouldn't be difficult," Honey pointed out. But everyone seemed to think that the job of welcoming the speaker should devolve upon her. So, outwardly smiling and inwardly quaking, Honey stood near the door and received several personal congratulations on having secured "her friend" for this last-minute occasion.

Half a dozen times she found herself explaining that Dr. Anston was "not exactly a friend." But as most people seemed to take the curious view that this meant their relationship had a greater rather than a lesser degree of intimacy, she gave up trying to put things right. Presently she saw a black Jaguar drive up and stop outside the hall, and half a minute later Dr. Anston got out.

Somewhat nervously Honey went down the path to the gate to greet him. He was hatless and, she had to admit, was looking quite extraordinarily handsome. When he shook hands with her she found herself thinking that it was the first time she had actually felt that famous hand around hers. It did not surprise her that the hand felt so strong, but the light delicacy of touch moved and intrigued her.

As they went up the path together he said, "By the way, what is your name?"

"Honey," she replied, taken somewhat off her guard.

"Am I expected to call you Honey?" Dr. Anston inquired with an amused glance.

"Oh no!" Honey was abashed. "No, I'm sorry. I thought you knew my other name, though of course there's no reason why you should. My name is really Enid Milward. But everyone calls me Honey, though why, I don't know."

" '*Mi chiamano Mimi, ma perche non so,*' " quoted Dr. Anston with an amazingly excellent Italian accent. Then they went into the crowded hall.

There was a tremendous rustle of interest, and Honey blushed under her golden tan at being coupled with Dr. Anston in this extraordinary and unexpected manner. However, she efficiently piloted him to the side of the platform, where Mrs. Turtle received him almost with open arms.

"So good of you!" She wrung him by the hand. "Just up the side stairs here. But wouldn't you like Honey to come onto the platform with you?"

"No!" was the explosive whisper from Honey.

"I would love Honey to accompany me," replied Dr. Anston clearly, on a note of quite horrid amusement. "But I think" he surveyed the formidable array of—chairmen and secretaries already assembled there. "—I think no arrangement has been made for that."

So Dr. Anston was ushered onto the platform on his own, and from the body of the hall Honey saw her mother greet him with all the charm at her disposal— which was a great deal.

There was a certain amount of rearrangement and whispered introductions, and then the doctor settled back in his chair and looked most amazingly at ease. The chairman's opening remarks were delivered, the minutes were read, and the group meeting was well under way.

CHAPTER TWO

HONEY was used to seeing Dr. Anston in the chill ano-
nymity of a surgeon's mask and overalls, and to feeling the tremendous authority of his presence in the
operating room, so there was something indescribably novel about his relaxed, almost indulgent air, as
he sat on the platform and looked around.

· She knew then that he was going to be a wonderful
success. Not, of course, that one could imagine his
being a real failure at anything, but somehow she had
thought he might not be able to take the full measure
of a setting so different from his usual one.

Nothing, however, could have been more suitable
to the demands of the occasion than the easy smile
with which he greeted the few sprightly remarks delivered by the chairman of Thorgay Institute, or the
charmingly attentive way he bent his handsome head
to catch some whispered inquiry from Mrs. Milward.

"She's asking him his Christian name now,"
thought Honey, half-horrified, half-intrigued.

But when he finally rose to speak, Honey found all
at once that her agitated flutterings had ceased to
exist. The most extraordinary sensation assailed her.
She discovered that the bond of shared work at St.
Margaret's was so strong upon her that all she could
think of was her immense pride in their surgeon, who
looked so easily master of the situation.

He might be nasty, cold and inhuman at times, if

she really cared to think back, but here Honey's recollections failed her. For, like everyone else in the hall, after the first few sentences, she yielded to the spell of a fascinating story, told in a voice of remarkable charm and flexibility.

Why, Honey asked herself bewilderedly, had she never before realized what a beautiful speaking voice he possessed? Or that there was a quite fascinating variety of expression in those unexpectedly light gray eyes and the strong, firm but humorous mouth?

"It's seeing him from quite a different angle, of course," she decided. But even this hardly seemed to provide an adequate explanation.

He spoke briefly of his early days, paying a graceful tribute to the Women's Institutes that he remembered. Then he went on to describe something of the drama, pathos and triumph of modern plastic surgery.

Even Miss Emms forgot to look as though she knew more than the speaker, as he described how, in this most experimental branch of surgery, the hope of today might well become the great discovery of tomorrow. And all the time he spoke with complete and imaginative understanding of the mental anguish that inevitably forms such a large part of the misfortune of disfigurement or deformity.

"*This* is why his patients love him," thought Honey. "What does his sarcastic manner count against such understanding? I've misjudged him, and I almost wish I could tell him so."

"You lucky girl," whispered sentimental old Mrs. Harridge, who was sitting beside her. "He's a wonderful man."

"Yes, isn't he?" whispered Honey back again. "But

I do know I'm lucky." Because she realized that, after all, that was just what she was—lucky to work under such a personality.

At the end there were even a few tears wiped away, and the applause was little short of deafening. The votes of thanks were expressed with a touch of real fervor that seemed in keeping with what Mrs. Milward gracefully described as a great occasion in the annals of Meadlands.

Mrs. Turtle at this moment stood up, rather red in the face with mingled emotion and nervousness, and said that she thought there ought to be a vote of thanks to Honey Milward for having obtained this sensationally good speaker at the last minute. And, as Dr. Anston bowed slightly, if a trifle ironically, in Honey's direction at this, there was a fresh round of applause. A good many ladies turned around to smile understandingly at her.

After that, tea, tasting very good even if it did come out of an urn, and lavish refreshments were handed around, and there was as much moving about as was possible in the congested condition of the hall. Dr. Anston, with an air of friendly informality that secretly astonished Honey, came down into the body of the hall and made himself very agreeable, though he skillfully fended off all requests by visiting chairmen to come and address their respective institutes. Yet he did it charmingly.

"My one and only appearance," he insisted with a smile, thereby filling Mrs. Milward's cup of pleasure to the brim. For, as every chairman and secretary knows, to obtain a good speaker is to taste the sweetness of triumph. But to obtain a good speaker who is unobtainable by others is tantamount to wearing the conqueror's laurels. She gasped with satisfaction.

"So kind of you to have made this one exception," murmured Mrs. Milward with what she hoped was smiling modesty.

"All thanks to Honey," remarked Mrs. Turtle approvingly.

"All thanks to Honey," agreed Dr. Anston, glancing at that young woman in a way that made her blush.

"We're all very fond of Honey, you know, Dr. Anston. We've seen her grow up," Mrs. Turtle explained. "And when we heard it was a special friend of hers who was coming to speak to us, we were quite excited."

"Was that what you heard?" he inquired mildly. And, although Honey made an attempt to put in a word here, Mrs. Turtle swept on.

"Indeed, yes! Miss Emms and I were just saying—"

But, at this point, Miss Emms struggled up to the group to speak for herself.

"An excellent speech, Dr. Anston." She shook him energetically by the hand. "The best speech we have had for seven or eight years." This took one back to Miss Emms's own years of office. "When I heard it was a special friend of Honey's who was coming, I was afraid there might have been a certain amount of partiality directing the choice. But, believe me, Dr. Anston, you did splendidly on your own merits."

He said he was so glad to hear this, and Miss Emms withdrew, evidently under the impression that she had made his afternoon. Others came up to add their quota of congratulations and approval. Eventually Miss Selby, the highly efficient secretary, insinuated herself between two broadly built figures and said in a confidential whisper, "It really isn't necessary for you or Honey to stay for the social half-hour, Dr. Anston. We do understand if you two want to get away on your own."

"Thank you," he said and eyed Honey with a rather dangerous glance. "Perhaps we should go."

"But Mother's expecting me to stay," Honey declared eagerly. "I didn't come with Dr. Anston, Miss Selby. I'm afraid there's some sort of mistake. You see—"

"No, no, dear." Miss Selby smiled, with what Honey found an almost nightmarish degree of understanding. "There's no mistake. Everyone understands very well, and I'm sure it was awfully good of you both to give up so much of your afternoon. You just slip away now, and I'll explain to your mother. She won't mind a bit."

Honey began to say something else, but her mother rang her bell at that moment and announced that Thorgay Institute was going to give a play.

"Now's your moment," said the efficient Miss Selby, wafting them both toward the door.

Just short of the doorway, however, Mrs. Harridge waylaid them, obviously determined to unburden herself of the happy speech she had been composing during the past ten minutes.

"Dr. Anston, you're a lucky man," she said, shaking the great surgeon by the hand. "There isn't a nicer girl than Honey this side of Forchester. But, mind you, she's a lucky girl too, and she knows it. I told her just now that I thought she was and, 'Mrs. Harridge,' she said, 'I know it!'"

"But I didn't mean—" began Honey desperately.

"Now," directed Miss Selby, like one starting the runners in a marathon race, and Honey somehow found herself outside the door in the company of Dr. Anston. For a moment Miss Selby's hand waved beneficently from the diminishing aperture. Then the door was closed, and Honey stood alone with a man who was no longer the charming, friendly lecturer of the group meeting, but the ice-cold surgeon she had once called a monster.

"And now, my very special friend," he said grimly, "I think you'd better come with me in my car and give me a few explanations."

With no more choice of action than a prisoner on the way to the scaffold, Honey was piloted along the path, handed into the black Jaguar, and installed in physical, if not mental, comfort beside Dr. Anston.

Then, still with no word from her, the car started. With a curious feeling of helplessness, she saw the familiar village street sliding by her, and a few minutes later they were out in the open country, heading she knew not where.

The only thing she did know was that the man beside her was waiting for an explanation of what had happened in the village hall.

"I can't begin to tell you how sorry I am—" she murmured timidly at last.

"You don't have to," he interrupted dryly. "You only have to explain how it all happened."

"But I don't know!" Honey cried. "Any more than you do."

"Oh, come, Miss Milward—" The mildness of his tone struck her as oddly dangerous. "You must have given them some sort of lead, surely."

"I certainly did not!" Honey retorted with a sudden

spurt of anger. "You don't suppose I liked having you foisted off on me as a particular friend, do you? I choose my friends with more discrimination," she added, rather inexcusably.

A curious silence followed this childish outburst. And then Honey said in a small voice, "I'm sorry."

He raised his eyebrows slightly, as though to say she should be.

"Truly, I can't tell you how the whole thing grew to such proportions," she said almost pleadingly. "But if you've practised in a country district, as you say, you must know as well as I do that it doesn't take more than a few words to touch off a whole train of gossip and misconception."

"Of course," he agreed coolly. "All I wanted to know was—who uttered those first few words?"

"I don't know," Honey insisted obstinately. But she turned cold suddenly as she remembered her mother's blithe assertions to Miss Emms that morning. "Half the people in the village have been trying to ma—I mean, pair me off—with someone, since I was about 16."

At that he turned his head for a moment and regarded her consideringly. "Yes," he agreed, somewhat enigmatically. "I suppose they would."

Honey's curiosity won over her annoyance and anxiety. "What do you mean by that, exactly?" she inquired.

"You don't need me to tell you that you are unusually pretty," he replied dryly. "An ideal choice for a vicarious romance."

Honey was struck dumb, and after a moment he went on, with a deliberation she thought quite fiendish. "I suppose they all think now that you and I have gone off to buy the ring. Well, what a predicament!"

"Some of them will, no doubt," agreed Honey, trying to match his coolness and failing. "But Mother will explain, I'm sure," she added the next moment, with anxious insistence.

"Think so?" He gave her a disturbing glance. "Your mother was one of those who greeted me, in a discreet whisper, of course, on the platform, as 'a special friend of Honey's.' "

The way he said "Honey" made it sound like some idiotic sobriquet, and Honey went a deep, soft pink.

"I'm dreadfully sorry about all this," she said with what courageous determination she could muster. "In spite of all my efforts to rid her of any such notion, I'm afraid Mother insisted on seeing you in the light of the romantic figure who saved the day. I think she must have been the first one to describe you as a friend of mine, though I never claimed such a thing. The rest was embroidered in an orgy of wishful thinking. But, believe me, you're no more furious about it all than I am," she concluded feelingly.

"I did not say that I'm furious about it," stated Dr. Anston enigmatically, in answer to all this apologizing.

"But—" she was completely put off her apologetic stroke "—of course you are!" she exclaimed indignantly, as though she needed to convince him of the fact.

"Oh, I don't know. I'm beginning to enjoy the situation," he declared carelessly. "I've never been engaged before. And certainly I never thought of becoming engaged to someone who regarded me as a monster."

Honey's color deepened once more, but with a sort

of desperate obstinacy she said, "I'm not going to apologize for that—nor take it back."

"I don't want you to," he assured her. "It would spoil the situation if you did." And then, before she could ask what on earth he meant by that, he went on, "You have a certain flair for saying unexpected and provocative things. What, for heaven's sake, did you say to the old lady who stopped us near the door and told me I was a lucky man?"

"A . . . a lucky man?" stammered Honey, seeing greater gulfs opening before her.

"Yes. 'Dr. Anston, You're a lucky man,'" quoted her companion, with terrifying accuracy. "'There isn't a nicer girl than Honey this side of Forchester. But, mind you, she's a lucky girl too, and she knows it. I told her so just now and she said, "Mrs. Somebody-or-other, I know it!"' Why did you claim to be a lucky girl, so far as I was concerned?" he inquired quite lightly, but with an underlying note in his voice that told her he meant to have a reply.

"It was all a mistake," Honey said desperately but inadequately, wondering if it would be any solution to her problem to throw herself out of the moving car to avoid further questioning. A moment's reflection, however, convinced her that she would merely find herself admitted to St. Margaret's as a special patient of Dr. Anston's, thus making her position ten times worse. So she gathered her wits and tried again. "When Mrs. Harridge whispered to me that I was a lucky girl, I thought she meant I was lucky to work for you."

"And to this you agreed emphatically?"

"I . . . yes," conceded Honey helplessly.

"Most gratifying," observed Dr. Anston. "I hadn't

realized that you considered yourself fortunate to work under me."

"I don't, in the ordinary way," retorted Honey, stung into another of those unfortunate home-truths. "Only this afternoon it was different."

"Why?" he wanted to know, this tone was the one he used when determinedly plumbing the depths of an over-confident student's meager knowledge.

There was a long moment's silence. Then Honey said, as though she could not help it, "This afternoon you sounded kind, warm and understanding. I saw you for a moment—I think we all did—as a man who put his knowledge, strength and genius at the disposal of suffering humanity, and asked nothing in return but that broken lives should be mended."

"I ask very handsome fees in return, if my patients can afford them," he retorted rather disagreeably. But, glancing at him, she thought he was not a little moved.

"Well," Honey said soberly, "the fact was that we were all carried away by what you said and the way you said it. If you want me to gratify you by the final admission, I suppose that, in some obscure way, I was proud to think I worked at the same hospital as you, and sometimes even under your direction."

She thought he might have been generous enough to reply quite seriously to that. But his tone was still determinedly mocking as he said, "And as a result of your momentary submission to an effective speech, you found yourself more or less engaged to me. Too bad."

"Oh, Dr. Anston!" Honey was genuinely shocked. "Don't exaggerate. It's all very embarrassing and annoying, I admit. But there's no question of your—

or our—I mean, there isn't anything that can't be determinedly explained away. As soon as I get home...."

"But I don't think I want it explained away," Dr. Anston said.

Honey blinked her gold-tipped lashes and swallowed hard.

"What did you say?" she asked timidly.

"What you thought I said," he assured her calmly. "I don't think I want our engagement explained away. It happens to suit me admirably."

"Happens to suit *you!*" The color rushed into Honey's cheeks once more. "And what about me? Suppose it doesn't suit me?"

"Oh, my dear Honey—" he said, and suddenly she found that it intrigued, as well as infuriated, her to have him call her "Honey" in that soft, amused tone of voice. "I would not, of course, have dreamed of involving you in such a situation on purpose. But since chance shall we say—?"

"It was chance!" Honey interjected, stung by the certainty that he still suspected her of pretending a friendship with him that did not exist, in order to cut a figure in her home village.

"Since chance," he agreed, "has dictated the position for us, I must repeat, although the phrase seems to annoy you, that the situation happens to suit me very well."

"But I don't know what you mean!", Anger and alarm struggled in Honey's voice. "How can it suit you to appear to be engaged to someone you don't like and who doesn't like you?"

"Is it really as emphatic as that?" He turned his head and smiled at her suddenly. For a moment she recaptured a slight degree of the afternoon's spell.

"I don't want to labor the point," she said and dropped her eyes. "But we certainly are not friends."

He did not reply to that. Instead he drew the car up before a pleasant-looking roadside restaurant and said, "Shall we go in and discuss this over tea? I don't expect you managed to get any more tea than I did, with all the congratulations and inquiries."

He took her consent for granted, which was Dr. Anston's way, of course, and presently they were seated in a long, cool panelled room, with a large teapot of "family" proportions in front of Honey. A profusion of cakes, scones, jam and cream was grouped enticingly on the table.

Honey, who possessed a healthy young appetite, began to remember that she had had a hasty and rather meager lunch. But, as she poured out the doctor's tea, she felt she must know what fate was hanging over her before she could really enjoy the good things. So, as she pushed the sugar bowl a little self-consciously toward him, she said. "Will you tell me if you were . . . if you were teasing me just now, or if you seriously meant that you thought you might—we might. . . ."

"My dear Honey, I am completely serious. I hope you don't mind my calling you Honey, since everyone else does. And, by the way, my name is John."

"Is it?" said Honey faintly, and there passed before her a confused vision of herself rushing up to him in the operating room and saying, "Oh, John!" while Sister fell in a dead faint.

"I shall have to explain my family background to you," he went on coolly. "My parents are dead, but I have one very charming, very determined, very managing sister. She is a good deal older than I am, and ever since she married extremely happily herself, it has been her one hope and ambition to see me in the same blessed condition. To her, any reasonably eligible bachelor constitutes a challenge. And a bachelor within her own family circle is something hardly to be borne."

He paused, and Honey fixed him with a beautiful but skeptical glance.

"Dr. Anston, are you asking me to believe that you're not a match for your own sister if it comes to a contest of wills?" she said with a touch of innocent irony.

"Ah, but you see, I'm fond of her," he retorted, with that quick and unexpectedly charming smile. "If it were merely a question of being crushing, I would—I know you will agree—be able to deal with the situation single-handedly. But, as it is, ever since I was about 22. . . ."

He paused again, perhaps at the gleam of speculative interest that had come into her eyes. "34," he said with apparent irrelevance.

"I beg your pardon?" Honey blushed.

"Not at all. It's customary to know the age of one's fiancé," he said, brushing that aside. "What I was saying was that, since about age 22 I have, with varying degrees of skill and tact, been avoiding the various plans my dear sister has made for me. During the past two years she and her husband have been abroad. I had hoped that by now she would regard me as either a hardened bachelor, or old enough to know my own affairs best."

"And doesn't she?" inquired Honey, interested in spite of herself.

"Unfortunately no."

"But if she's living abroad, as you say, I don't see that she can constitute a particular menace to your bachelor state."

"Ah, but she is coming home on a visit in the next few weeks."

"She may have changed her views by now. You never know."

"I'm afraid I do know," he corrected regretfully. "That's just my difficulty. She has written to say that she has met the very woman for me. In fact, she describes her in terms of menacing enthusiasm. And she adds the melancholy fact that they are traveling to England on the same boat and will be seeing a great deal of each other while my sister is here."

Honey was uneasily silent, and after a moment Dr. Anston went on reflectively, "It's a gloomy prospect and will entirely spoil a meeting I was anticipating with so much pleasure. On the other hand, of course, if I were already engaged when my sister landed. . . ."

"Dr. Anston, it's a preposterous idea!"

"My sister will be here for only six months," he remarked as though to himself. "After that, she and her husband will be returning to the States, where he has extensive business interests."

This time the silence was a longer one. But then Honey said, with ruthless determination, "I'm sorry, but I really can't regard this as a serious predicament. Certainly not one that would justify such a fantastic remedy."

"Serious is a relative term, Honey," he replied with that half-lazy, half-mischievous smile, which made her wonder if he had really been laughing at her all the time. "And it has so much to do with the viewpoint of the person concerned. I suppose some people would not have realized that your mother's predicament this morning was at all serious."

"My mother's predicament? Oh!" Suddenly, and with great clarity, she remembered how he had come unhesitatingly to their rescue over the dreadful crisis of the missing speaker. "But that's different!" she said earnestly. And then immediately wondered if his help on that occasion constituted a moral claim to her assistance now.

"Well, if you say it's different, it is," he agreed, thereby making her feel that perhaps she was being ungenerous and ungrateful.

"Dr. Anston—" her voice took on an almost pleading note,"— you do see, don't you, that I can't be engaged to you? It's an unheard of suggestion!"

"But, my dear, you are, more or less, in the minds of several people who know you well," he reminded her, with what she could not help feeling was a certain degree of malicious enjoyment.

"Not irrevocably so," Honey countered quickly.

"No. Nothing is irrevocable," he agreed. "But then this engagement would not be irrevocable either. My sister would be leaving England just about the time, I suppose, when you would be completing your training at St. Margaret's. I take it you were not planning to stay on at the hospital after your third year?"

"I don't think so." Honey conceded.

"Very well, then. The situation would solve itself," he declared, with a composure that she thought excessive.

"I don't see quite how." She stared at the teapot and wondered if her voice sounded as uncertain to him as it did to her.

"Don't you?" he said, kindly but with an alarming degree of firmness. "As I see it, you would leave the hospital and go to London or into private nursing, or whatever you originally intended. There would be a certain amount of gossip and speculation still, perhaps, on the days when I visited St. Margaret's. But, after a while, it would all die a natural death, with no inconvenience to you and very little to me. The advantage of the whole scheme would be that I would have thoroughly enjoyed my sister's visit, free from any well-intended interference on her part."

Honey was silent, though she felt instinctively that it was a weakness even to appear to consider his proposition. For some reason she felt struck dumb.

"Do you think it would be necessary to admit to an engagement at the hospital?" she asked at last.

"Oh certainly!"

"Wouldn't it be sufficient if we just pretended to your sister? I could come and meet her and. . . ."

"No, no." He dismissed such faint-hearted tactics with good-humored impatience. "If we do the thing at all, we must do it properly. It would be asking for trouble and complications if we posed as an engaged couple in one part of our lives and not in another."

Honey reluctantly saw the force of that, but still hesitated on the brink of what seemed to her an extraordinarily perilous decision.

"For six months only?" she said at last.

"Possibly a little less," he replied encouragingly. "For the length of my sister's stay in this country."

"And you really mean that this would be a great help to you?"

"An enormous help," he assured her gravely. "As I said earlier, it would never have occurred to me to invent such a situation. But, since it has been more or less forced upon us, I am more than willing to accept it. If you agree," he added politely.

In actual words, the final qualification sounded as though she still had some choice in the matter. But Honey had an inner conviction that it was little more than a figure of speech. Right from the beginning, she had known in her heart that if Dr. Anston wanted something, the chances were 100 to one against his failing to get it.

And, incredible though it might seem, he wanted to be engaged to her. Or, at least, to appear to be engaged to her.

"Very well," she said finally, her tone carrying something between resignation and bravado. "I can't deny that I was profoundly thankful for your help this morning, and I suppose it would be ungrateful not to acknowledge a sort of moral claim on my help now."

"I don't think I would put it that way," he said mildly. "I did your mother that small favor without any thought of putting either of you under an obligation. It's more that, through good or ill fortune, as one cares to look at it, this situation has arisen and—"

"We won't split hairs about it," interrupted Honey, aware that, if they discussed it much longer, her courage would fail her. "If you truly want my help in this fantastic form, then I'll—" she swallowed "—do my best. But please keep it all as academic as possible."

Her choice of words seemed to amuse him a good deal. "I don't know that one can be academically engaged, Honey," he said. "But at least I will undertake to steer you clear of too many complications."

A typically arrogant Anston claim, Honey thought crossly. But she had accepted now, and she would see the situation through to the best of her ability. Even though a voice inside her had already begun to question her decision. Where would such a situation lead to? It seemed far-fetched and almost dangerous in some half-sensed way. But she had given him her word. There was no getting out of it!

CHAPTER THREE

PRESENTLY Dr. Anston remarked that perhaps it was time they went home and told Honey's parents their news. And, although the practical finality of that nearly made her panic, Honey supposed that whether an engagement were real or pretended, one had to go through the form of telling one's parents at an early stage in proceedings.

By the time they returned to Meadlands, all the buses had departed with their satisfied loads, the village hall was being stripped of its floral decorations, and a tired but triumphant Mrs. Milward was preparing to relax and spend a quiet evening.

In her pleasant, restful living room, Honey and Dr. Anston came to her with their news.

At first it was a little difficult to make her understand that her daughter had really become engaged, although, as she told her husband afterward, it had been the sort of day on which almost anything could happen.

But when she had finally grasped the glad tidings, she jumped up, tired though she was, and embraced her child, with all the enthusiasm that was left in her after the group meeting.

"How perfectly, perfectly wonderful, Honey darling!" And then, turning to the smiling Dr.

Anston, she added, "And although I have only just met you, John, I feel that I already know you well."

Honey secretly thought her mother was much too ready with her "John"—a term that she herself had not managed to apply to him. But worse was to follow, for her mother called the famous surgeon "My dear boy" and kissed him. Which was, again, more than her daughter had dreamed of doing.

"I suppose it's all rather sudden, since Honey never mentioned you until this morning," said Mrs. Milward, looking at her proposed son-in-law pensively. "But you must have known each other at the hospital for some while."

"That's true," he agreed, returning her kiss with apparent enjoyment. "But it wasn't until today that I managed to persuade Honey to really take me seriously."

"Imagine that!" Mrs. Milward smiled happily at the pair of them. "And to think that if your aunt hadn't let us down, and Honey hadn't bravely offered to go over and interview her, this might never have happened."

"It's a solemn thought," said Dr. Anston, while Honey could find no answer to the undoubted truth of her mother's statement.

"Honey dear, I'm so happy for you." Her mother hugged and kissed her again, and at the same time managed to whisper, "He's a man in a thousand, darling. I could tell that from his talk."

Honey smiled, returned the kiss and tried to look like a happily engaged girl.

"You must stay to dinner, of course," Mrs. Milward said as she turned back to him, "and have a talk with Honey's father. Honey dear, I'm sure you want to go and change into something really festive and pretty for the occasion."

So Honey, borne along now on what seemed to her an inevitable tide, went upstairs to her room. She took from her wardrobe the cream colored dress with the powdering of gold spots, which was, she was sure, what her mother had had in mind. As she put it on, brushed her shining hair, and touched her lips with red, she kept on telling herself that it was quite impossible to go on with this fantastic situation.

But, when she looked at herself in the full-length mirror and saw a fair-haired girl with thoughtful dark eyes and a mischievous curve to her mouth, she began to have the strange feeling that there was something exciting and challenging in the idea of playing this masquerade out with John Anston, of all people.

He should not have it all his own way! For in spite of all this talk about his match-making sister, Honey could not help thinking that he was more than half-prompted by a malicious desire to punish her; both for her strictures on him and for what he regarded as her presumptuous pretence of an intimate friendship between them.

Well, she would have some fun too. She was not going to be the poor little victim of Dr. Anston's mocking ingenuity. And, with a swirl of her ivory skirt and a gay, impudent wave to her reflection, Honey ran downstairs to deal with her new fiancé.

As she came downstairs, he was standing in the hall talking to her father. Both of them had their backs to her, her father pointing out something framed in the open front doorway. Afterward she was not quite sure if it was her new, reckless mood that prompted her, or if she really only wanted to play her part well in front of her father. At any rate, she jumped the last two stairs and ran across the hall, to cast her arms around Dr. Anston from behind and say, "I'm ready, John! How do you like my dress?"

Even before he turned to look at her, she knew she had administered a shock. There was a sort of fierce enjoyment in the fact that, for once, *she* had startled *him*.

Then, as her father said, "Well, Honey, this is great news." Dr. Anston turned in the circle of her arms and lifted her clear off the ground.

"You look wonderful, my darling," he said and kissed her deliberately on her lips as he set her down again.

Somehow she had not expected quite such cooperation. Something witty and flippant would have been more in character. And for a moment Honey was hard put to answer her father's questions and congratulations coherently.

But coherence is not what is expected of a newly engaged daughter, and her father evidently saw nothing wrong. He kissed her, said she was a secretive child to have kept all this to herself, and then they all went in to dinner. For good or ill, Mrs. Milward took over the direction of the conversation.

Inevitably, this ranged to future plans. Honey found herself discussing the length of her engagement to Dr. Anston, the design of her wedding dress, and the place where she was likely to live when she set up house with him.

If, she told herself, she had realized to what refinements of anxiety and embarrassment she was committing herself when she took this thing on, she would never have consented to go through such an involved farce.

But then she looked across the table at Dr. Anston, his handsome head bent a trifle deferentially toward her mother, and again the feeling came over her that, in some terrifying but exciting way, this was an experience she would not have missed.

It seemed that they must both have played their parts well, for neither of her parents appeared to notice anything unusual in their attitude. It was true that, toward the end of dinner, Mrs. Milward's attention wandered once or twice. But this was explained when, as they rose from the table, she said with elaborate carelessness, "I think I should telephone Miss Emms about one or two things that happened this afternoon."

"She knows about Honey," interjected her husband cryptically.

"Knows about Honey!" Mrs. Milward actually flushed with annoyance. "What do you mean? She can't know about Honey. We've only just heard the news ourselves."

"Selina Emms has a private receiving set concealed in her hat," declared Mr. Milward solemnly. "Or possesses some sixth sense that tells her about events just a short while before they occur. When I stopped at the post office on my way home, she accosted me, strictly in the social sense of the word, of course, and said she thought Honey had chosen very well and that doctors always made such steady husbands." He grinned ruefully at his wife.

"But," cried Mrs. Milward, greatly chagrined, "didn't you ask her what she meant?"

"No, of course not. I would still be there now, if I had," replied her husband. And, shaking out the pages of his evening newspaper, he turned to the section headed, "Today on the Stock Exchange," which is so very absorbing or so very boring, according to one's degree of ignorance.

After a moment's thought, Mrs. Milward still elected to go and telephone Miss Emms. Dr. Anston had ample opportunity to say quietly to Honey, "You see? It would have been almost impossible to talk ourselves out of it anyway."

"Do you think," inquired Honey in the same low tones, "that it will be any easier in six months: time?"

Even he had no very convincing answer to this. So he laughed and kissed the tip of her ear instead, which might or might not have been for her father's benefit.

It was a very curious sort of evening, but not entirely without its own particular sense of enjoyment. To Honey it was as though she had suddenly discovered how to walk a tightrope and was now committed to the half-terrifying, half-exhilarating experience of doing so.

But toward the end she began to feel a certain degree of strain and was not sorry when Dr. Anston said that he had no intention of keeping them all up late after what must have been an exhausting day.

"I have to return to London tomorrow, Honey,"

he said, "and I shall not be back until Thursday, when, of course, I shall be operating at St. Margaret's as usual. Would you care to come with me and choose your ring?"

Slightly off her guard now that she was feeling tired, Honey nearly fell into the trap of remarking that, in the circumstances, almost any ring would do. But recovering herself in time, she said very sweetly that she was sure John would choose something she would like.

"Besides, you'll be busy all day at your London hospital on Tuesday and Wednesday," she pointed out. "I think I'll stay quietly at home and enjoy my few days' leave."

"Oh, darling!" her mother rushed eagerly into the discussion. "Do go if you want to. Now that this has happened, we don't expect to keep you selfishly to ourselves. And one is only engaged once—or, at least, one hopes so."

At the singular inappropriateness of this observation, Honey had difficulty not meeting Dr. Anston's humorous glance. But she contrived to go on looking sweet and firm. And, having repeated that she preferred not to go to London at this moment, she walked with him to the gate, because this appeared to be what her mother, at least, expected.

"An admirable performance," he declared "on the part of both of us."

"I'm glad you think so," replied Honey a trifle grimly. "But I wish I knew exactly where all this is leading us."

"Don't worry," he told her lightly. "We've taken the first and worst hurdle, and taken it well."

Then he kissed her good night. She thought that a little excessive, even though they were in view of the house and possibly of her mother.

On her return to the house, she naturally had to receive further congratulatory comments from her parents. Her father seemed as pleased as her mother with what ironically he called her choice.

"He's a very good type, my dear, very good," he assured a secretly dissenting Honey. "You and your mother can rejoice in the romantic side of this match, if you like. But what pleases me is that he's a fine man, and in a very good social and financial position."

"Yes, of course, these things do matter," murmured Honey, trying to look starry-eyed and failing. "But now I'm just exhausted with all the excitement. I . . . I think I'll go to bed."

"Do, darling!" Her mother kissed her fondly. "I've never known such a day in the whole of my life. Not *ever*."

"What about the day you became engaged to me?" inquired her husband teasingly.

"Oh, well." Mrs. Milward looked pensive and smiled in the lovely way that made her look like Honey's elder sister. "That was pretty thrilling too. But there was no triumphant group meeting beforehand," she recalled suddenly. "No. This is the day of days, isn't it, Honey dear?"

"Honey dear" said, with what conviction she could, that it was indeed the day of days. Then she finally escaped to her room, telling herself that at any rate during John's two days' absence she could probably take things more quietly.

In this, however, she was mistaken.

By lunchtime of the following day, there were few people left in Meadlands who did not know that Honey Milward was engaged to that handsome surgeon who had saved the day with his brilliant lecture at the W.I. group meeting.

"It's like something in a book," cried sentimental little Miss Morris at the post office, when Honey entered, unsuspectingly, to buy some stamps. "And everyone says he looks like a movie star."

"I don't think he would care for the comparison himself," Honey said truthfully.

"Oh, I only mean in looks." Slightly shocked, Miss Morris strove to reassure Honey. "Nothing to do with their attitude to marriage, of course. I'm sure he is most faithful and reliable. Doctors always are."

Honey said she was glad Miss Morris thought so and hurried out to escape further comment. But, wherever she went, smiles and glances followed her. She was even aware that curtains in front windows quivered suggestively as she walked past.

"I don't know why everyone should be quite so interested," she remarked a trifle crossly to her mother.

"Oh, but, darling, all the world loves a lover," Mrs. Milward reminded her. And then, a little as though she thought that might be casting aspersions of Dr. Anston's motives, she added hastily, "Meaning an engagement and a wedding, of course."

"All the same, I could have done with a bit less audience participation and rather more privacy," Honey said with a sigh. "But I suppose it can't be helped."

The climax, however, was reached the following day, when a Rolls-Royce drew up outside the Milwards' house. Out stepped Madame Seroni, obviously to pay a state visit.

Her object was two-fold as she explained with inoffensive candor. She had come first to apologize for her non-appearance at the meeting, and then to satisfy a most lively curiosity as to the girl who had succeeded in capturing her somewhat elusive nephew.

She was a large, handsome woman, with a bosom designed by nature for the display of diamonds. But she was also kind and amusing, and quite prepared to like Honey on sight.

"No wonder he fell in love with you, dear child," she said, regarding Honey with favor, and speaking in a beautiful, mellow voice that penetrated without effort to every corner of the room. "You're the prettiest thing I've seen in years."

Honey naturally blushed a little at this and, smiling, said she was glad Madame Seroni was pleased with John's choice.

"*Very* pleased," Madame Seroni repeated emphatically. "And it was high time he married, in any case. No sort of life for any man, living in bachelor's apartments, with no interest in life but making people's faces look more attractive than God meant them to be."

This view of plastic surgery was a novel one to Honey. But she smiled again and said very convincingly that she hoped she would make John happy.

"Make him happy? See that he makes you happy," retorted Madame Seroni firmly. "Begin as

51

you are going on, my dear. That's a sound rule in any undertaking. Even marriage," she added, apparently putting that low down on the list.

Honey thought of the way in which John was regarded at St. Margaret's and quaked in the role now cast for her.

"But he is a good boy," went on Madame Seroni, apparently finding nothing incongruous in this way of describing the Anston legend. "And I was touched and delighted to hear how happy he sounded when he gave me the good news over the telephone yesterday."

"Did he sound happy?" inquired Honey curiously.

"Well, of course, dear child. Surely that doesn't surprise you?" And her visitor laughed in a beautiful, but somewhat over-life-sized way.

"Not really. No," Honey murmured.

Then Madame Seroni demanded to see her ring, and Honey had to explain that this was being brought from London the following day.

"I'm meeting John in Forchester tomorrow evening," she explained. "I'm on leave from the hospital myself, but he, of course, will be operating there most of the day. We shall meet each other afterward."

"But I can't imagine that you won't make an excuse to slip into the place first to let all your friends know the news." Honey's visitor smiled at her indulgently. "Nurses adore a bit of romantic gossip, don't they? And, of *course*, you will want to tell them all about your engagement yourself."

"I think not," said Honey, who was secretly unnerved every time she thought of trying to explain to Barbara and the others how it was that, far from hating Dr. Anston, as they all supposed, she had suddenly become engaged to him.

"Not?" Madame Seroni raised expressive eyebrows amusedly. "Don't tell me you're self-conscious about capturing the most eligible bachelor in the hospital?"

"Oh, no. Not at all," said Honey, hastily if untruthfully. "It's just that I think I shall leave it to John to say what he thinks best. And by the time I return on Sunday night, I expect everyone will have heard the news."

Madame Seroni said that she thought Honey was doing herself out of a good deal of the fun attached to an engagement, but that it was entirely her own business. Then she prepared to make her departure in an atmosphere of the greatest friendliness.

"She's charming, my dear, absolutely charming," she assured Mrs. Milward, as though Honey were not there. "A little shy, perhaps, but that's a good fault these days." And then she made a splendid exit, assisted by a very attentive chauffeur ready to spread a fur rug over her knees, before driving off in her Rolls-Royce.

"Which does help, of course," as Mrs. Milward cryptically remarked.

"She's nice," said Honey. "I like her. Even if she did let us down over the W.I. group meeting."

"And, in view of what happened afterward, I think it's a good thing she did," declared Mrs. Milward, in a burst of generosity and forgiveness.

Honey could not bring herself to echo this sentiment, and there was a moment's silence.

"Why did she think you shy, dear?" asked Mrs.

Milward who, to tell the truth, had never noticed this one trait in her usually happy and friendly child.

"Oh, I think it was just because I chose not to go and break the news of my engagement myself at the hospital," Honey said rather uncomfortably. "But it's much better if John does it."

"Do you think so?" Her mother looked pensive. "I think most girls like to give quite such radiant news themselves."

"Not," Honey stated firmly, "to people like Sister or Matron."

"Well no. Perhaps not to them," Mrs. Milward conceded. "But to your few chosen intimates."

"That sort of news doesn't stop short at one's few chosen intimates in hospital," Honey assured her mother. "The report would be around the place in no time. No, much the best thing is to leave it to Dr. Anston—John, I mean. He'll know just how to put it to Matron. At least, I hope he will," she added gloomily. "Then, by the time I go on duty on Monday morning, most people will have become used to the situation."

But nothing turned out the way Honey had planned. For, hardly had this conversation ended when the telephone rang. On answering its summons, Honey discovered that no less a person than Matron wished to speak to her.

For a ridiculous and panic-stricken moment, Honey thought Matron must have heard of her engagement and be about to reprimand her for something she regarded as a tasteless escapade. But common sense and Matron's next words dispelled that idea.

"I am really sorry to have to break in on your week's leave, Nurse," she said, in a tone as nearly apologetic as is suitable between a matron and a third-year nurse. "I'm afraid this is the penalty of living within easy reach of your work."

"That's quite all right, Matron." In her relief at the discovery that this conversation had nothing to do with her engagement, Honey sounded almost as though she had just been sitting by the telephone waiting for her holiday to be interrupted by the call of duty.

"The trouble is that we have had several cases of flu on the operating room staff and are desperately short-handed. I wonder if it would be interfering with any very special plans of yours if I asked you to be on duty tomorrow morning and take the rest of your leave later?"

"Why, of course I will, Matron," said Honey, still under the spell of relief. "I'll come back into the hospital tonight and be ready for duty tomorrow morning as usual."

"Thank you very much Nurse. It would be a great help. Dr. Anston will be operating in Room Two tomorrow, and, as you know, he does not suffer inexperienced pros gladly."

It was the nearest to a humorous unbending ever achieved by Matron in their relationship so far, and Honey gave a flattered little laugh.

"I'll be there, Matron. I promise," she said.

Not until she had hung up the receiver did she realize how awkwardly her personal situation had become. Her next meeting with Dr. Anston would not be as his fiancée, outside the hospital, but as a nurse in a place where his word was law.

55

"It doesn't matter, really," she tried to tell herself. But she knew very well that it mattered greatly. For one thing, none of the explanations of her new position would have been made for her. She would probably have to make them for herself. And then John would not even be expecting her. When he saw her, he would think. . . .

Oh, well, she didn't care what he would think, she assured herself. And, anyway, he might possibly not even recognize her if he saw her in a mask and gown; particularly as he would be thinking of her, if he thought of her at all, as safely at home in Meadlands.

Her mother was a good deal disappointed to hear that Honey was leaving them that evening, but she had long ago become resigned to the fact that nursing duties must come before everything else.

"And anyway," she said, recalling a most consoling fact, "it will be useful to have a few days' leave in hand. You're sure to need some time for trousseau buying and that sort of thing, quite apart from wanting an occasional day with John sometimes outside the hospital."

To this Honey somewhat doubtfully answered, "Yes," and went away to pack her case.

She supposed, as she folded dresses and skirts, that she was, in some degree, relieved to be going away from home. Not that she loved it any the less. But it is extraordinarily difficult to keep up an elaborate pretence with the people one knows and loves best.

"I couldn't have done it at all if Michael had been here," she decided, with a nostalgic thought for her elder brother. He would, she could not help reflecting, have probably extricated her in some way from her dilemma, if he had been home.

"He just wouldn't have let Dr. Anston make this ridiculous arrangement," Honey thought.

And then she stood for quite a long time, staring out of the window into the garden, trying to decide just how relieved she would be if Michael were to appear suddenly on the scene and undo all the mischief of the last few days.

"He couldn't exactly put back the clock, of course," she told herself. "There would always be this extraordinary incident between John and me. But I don't know that I would mind that so much. One couldn't ever again be dead scared of a man to whom one had been engaged. Even if the engagement were bogus."

But at this point the whole thing became so complicated in her own mind, and the motives and reactions so entirely inexplicable, that she abandoned any further attempt to disentangle the situation and completed her packing instead. Her mother accompanied her to the bus stop that evening, where, to Honey's secret irritation and her mother's mingled pleasure and annoyance, Miss Emms was also waiting for the Forchester bus.

"Well, Honey," she said, in the manner of one who had a special right both to question and advise, "where are you off to now?"

Honey explained about being recalled to the hospital, and Mrs. Milward quickly added a few words, calculated to give the impression that St. Margaret's had simply found that it could not manage without Honey's help.

"So you'll be working with that young man of

57

yours in the same operating room?" said Miss Emms. Her manner was calculated to give the impression that, famous surgeon or not, Dr. Anston was merely a promising beginner, in her eyes, and that the biggest moment in his life so far had probably been when she had expressed approval of him at the group meeting.

"I've been working the same operating room as Dr. Anston for sometime," Honey explained mildly, pressing her mother's arm warningly to stop her from rushing into a provocative reply.

"Well, don't become so absorbed in each other, the pair of you, that you forget about the wretched patient," admonished Miss Emms.

"We never forget about the patient at St. Margaret's," replied Honey coldly. Fortunately the bus came into sight at that moment, so there was no knowing what Mrs. Milward might have said, in angry defence of her daughter, her future son-in-law (as she fondly believed), and the hospital where they both worked.

"Goodbye, darling." Honey's mother kissed her and found time to whisper, "Keep your temper if you can. Though *how* you will, I don't know."

"I'll be all right," replied Honey, smiling, as she returned her mother's kiss.

Then she climbed into the bus, in the wake of Miss Emms's quite broad beam, and hauled in her case after her. Unfortunately, at this time in the evening, there were not many passengers traveling. So Honey had to sit beside Miss Emms, and listen, with what patience and courtesy she could, to an account of the full career of a brilliant woman surgeon whom Miss Emms had once known.

"There's no doubt, of course, that when you do get a good woman surgeon she's way in front of any man," Miss Emms stated authoritatively. "Much more imaginative, much more conscientious, and altogether more reliable."

And, so contrary is human nature, that Honey was surprised to hear herself retort, with some warmth, that *no* surgeon, man or woman, was more imaginative, conscientious or reliable than Dr. Anston.

"Well, well, you're prejudiced, I expect," said Miss Emms, with a not unkindly chuckle.

"I am not prejudiced! In fact. . . ."

But, by a special dispensation of Providence, Miss Emms realized just then that she had reached her stop. So she said goodbye to Honey and disembarked, leaving that distracted sham-fiancée thinking how very, very nearly she had told Miss Emms that she simply couldn't stand Dr. Anston.

Honey had only ten minutes more of her own journey left. During that time she tried to compose her thoughts and arrive at some state of mind suitable to her new situation. But she had made little progress toward that desirable end when the bus stopped outside the nurses' residence.

"St. Margaret's!" shouted the conductor, and in a friendly way helped Honey to lift down her case from the bus. Then the bus went on, and Honey walked the last few paces to the block that was the nurses' residence.

No longer was she Honey Milward, the popular daughter of the Chairman of Meadlands Women's Institute. She was Nurse Milward, returning to the life in which John Anston was a remote, Olympian figure, to whom one said, "Yes, sir," and, very, very rarely, "No, sir." In this familiar setting, she reflected wryly, he would probably all but ignore her. Unless, of course, he had decided to play his role as doting fiancé to the hilt. She repressed the leaping thought: she rather hoped he would!

CHAPTER FOUR

So deeply was Honey under the influence of the events of the past few days that she felt, as she reentered the residence, that she must surely carry some evidence of her experiences on her face.

But no one commented or questioned. No one even glanced at her with covert interest as she checked in at the entry desk. And, when she arrived at the upper corridor where she and Barbara and several others of her acquaintance had their rooms, a passing nurse greeted her with no more than, "Hello, are you another one summoned back from leave? Well, I suppose you weren't doing anything special, as you were just at home."

For a moment Honey toyed with the idea of saying, "I was only getting engaged to Dr. Anston." But her courage failed her, particularly as the speaker was one of those who had witnessed Dr. Anston's original rebuke to her. So she murmured falsely that she had not been doing anything special and went on to her own room.

Here Barbara, recently off duty, joined her almost immediately. Being a much more intimate friend than the other nurse, she naturally asked more detailed questions about Honey's affairs.

"You say Matron herself telephoned for you? My, you should feel flattered! She must know you as the girl who stood up to Dr. Anston," declared Barbara.

"Oh, I don't expect so," replied Honey uncomfortably.

"I wouldn't worry," said Barbara kindly, mistaking the reason for Honey's subdued tone. "I don't expect you'll be much longer on operating room duty. And then you'll hardly ever see Dr. Anston and can forget all about his having had his knife in you."

"Oh, not really—no!" exclaimed Honey somewhat incoherently, for it was unnerving to be plunged immediately into the necessity of explaining the inexplicable.

"What do you mean?" Barbara looked surprised. "You surely don't mean to brood over the fact that he was beastly to you?"

"Oh no!" cried Honey again, feeling that she was slipping farther and farther into the bog of misunderstanding. "I meant. . . ." She stopped and then said with resolution, "Barbara, something happened while I was at home on leave."

Arrested by her tone, Barbara stared at her. Then her eyes widened incredulously.

"You mean in connection with Dr. Anston?" Honey nodded.

"He didn't make a private complaint about you? Come to your home or something?"

"No, of course not!" said Honey crossly, because it was becoming increasingly clear to her that she would not be able to break her news with less than a thunderclap. She swallowed and blurted out, "I mean that he asked me to marry him."

"He—?" Barbara took off her cap in a dazed way and sat down slowly on the side of the bed. "Say that again."

Honey said it again, but rather timidly.

"I don't understand. We are talking of *our* Dr. Anston, aren't we?" said Barbara almost pleadingly.

"Yes, of course."

"And he truly and seriously asked you to marry him?"

"Yes," said Honey, hoping her recording angel was not listening.

"But . . . what did you *say?*"

"I said 'yes,'" stated Honey, greatly simplifying all that she really had said.

"You. . . . Look here, am I crazy or are you?" inquired Barbara.

But before Honey could reply, an over-bright colleague called Peters put her head in and, on hearing this leading question, naturally said, "Both of you, I expect." Then, seeing Barbara's queer expression, she came farther into the room and asked curiously, "Is anything the matter?"

"No," said Barbara. "Nothing at all. Except that Milward has just got engaged to Dr. Anston."

At this, Peters, who should really have been a gossip writer and not a nurse, gave a squeal of delighted amusement and rushed out into the corridor, presumably to spread the glad and sensational tidings.

"I'm frightfully sorry." Barbara looked remorsefully at Honey. "I forgot what a tattler Peters is."

"It doesn't matter. She's probably saved me a lot of embarassing explanations," Honey replied. "It's not a bad idea to let everyone know at once."

Barbara glanced at her again, as though she no longer knew quite what to make of her once familiar companion. But before she could say any more, the first of the eager news-seekers arrived.

"Milward, what on earth is this story?" They

crowded into the open doorway of her room, amused, intrigued, congratulatory, very happy to have such an entrancing variant on hospital life at the end of a dull day.

"It's quite true." Barbara obligingly spoke up for Honey, who was slightly overcome by the sensation she was causing. "Honey's just told me herself. But if you want to know how it all came about, your guess is as good as mine. I thought you couldn't bear him, Honey," she added, her curiosity getting the better of her desire to shield her friend from too much questioning.

"Well, I was wrong." Honey colored, but made a great effort to appear like one who was both happy and amused about her own past blindness. "I met him outside hospital surroundings, so. . . ."

"How?" inquired Peters, now returned to the scene and looking as though she might produce a pencil and notebook at any moment.

Honey gave them a brief but, as she warmed to her task, amusing account of how she had induced Dr. Anston to save the show at the W.I. group meeting. Everyone enjoyed this, laughed a great deal and began to find the whole story not so entirely incredible.

"And then," said Honey, wisely sticking to the true facts, even though her interpretation of them was a trifle free, "he took me out in the car, gave me tea, asked me to bury the hatchet. Suddenly we found ourselves engaged."

"Just like that?" Barbara looked impressed.

"More or less," Honey asserted firmly. "There were a few intermediate steps, maybe."

Everyone said it was the most amazing thing they

had ever heard, though most of them agreed that it was quite delightful. Morgan, who was sentimental and had once been caught reading a romance while on night duty, added that it just showed how near love and hate were.

To all of which Honey found little to say. But as everyone felt she must really be very complex indeed to have achieved all this, it seemed quite in character for her to sit there smiling and apparently thinking her own thoughts.

"When are you going to tell Sister?" asked Peters. At that a solemn silence fell. For Sister was a formidable lady with, by virtue of her position, a sort of vested interest in surgeons that she did not like challenged. Immensely efficient herself, she tended to think poorly of nurses who were less than fully qualified, and would have preferred the godlike creatures who operated not even to say "Good morning" to the nurses. It would be hard for her to accept the fact that her favorite, Dr. Anston, should so far have forgotten himself as actually to become engaged to one.

"I shall leave John to tell her himself," replied Honey with admirable composure.

"Who?" asked Peters. And when it dawned on them that Honey was thus referring to the unapproachable Dr. Anston, everyone looked at her with a sort of awed respect she found difficult to sustain.

Questions were then asked about the ring, the length of engagement, and whether or not Honey intended to be married in the hospital chapel. And although the discussion of such details made Honey feel nervous and as though, literally and figuratively, she no longer had her feet on the ground, the truth was that she was now getting used to her situation. At least, she told herself, she had taken the difficult hurdle of the first announcement.

By the time the others scattered reluctantly to their own rooms once more, everyone had completely accepted the fact that Milward was engaged to Dr. Anston.

Next morning, the irresistible routine of hospital life claimed Honey so ruthlessly that she had tumbled out of bed at the sound of her alarm clock and was half-dressed before she clearly recalled her new status as the fiancée of Dr. Anston. And when she did so, the discovery disconcerted rather than gratified her.

For the queer thing was that, as she belted her uniform aound her trim waist, she somehow also put on the full identity of Nurse Milward and shed that of Honey. She had then the disconcerting experience of seeing recent events as Sister, for instance, would see them. And she could not help feeling that, after all, it was really very presumptuous of her to have become engaged to Dr. Anston, whatever the circumstances might be.

However, there was nothing she could do about it now. So, together with all the other nurses who were going on duty at the same time, she hurried down to breakfast, and then later went along to the operating room, trying to pretend to herself that this was just a day like any other day.

In company with a rather nervous and inexperienced nurse whom she hardly knew, Honey set about the familiar work of laying up the instrument trolleys. In the ordinary way, she was able to concentrate on this type of work to the exclusion of everything else, and even Sister had once implied, though not actually stated, that Honey was especially careful and reliable.

Every surgeon has certain favorite instruments, as a conductor may have a favorite baton. It was Honey's special pride that, in addition to knowing everything it was necessary to know about the routine laying up of an instrument trolley, she had a card-index knowledge of the methods and preferences of the surgeons for whom she worked.

Consequently, she secretly felt a good deal annoyed when, on that particular morning, Sister looked into the sterilizing room and said, "Please see that everything is completely in order for Dr. Anston. You know he doesn't suffer errors gladly."

"Yes, Sister," said Honey meekly at what she considered to be a most unnecessary admonition.

"Did you ever make a mistake?" inquired the nurse hopefully, when Sister had vanished into her adjoining office.

"No. Not about instruments, I mean," Honey said briefly.

"But you had an awful argument once with Dr. Anston, didn't you?" continued the newcomer respectfully.

"Not really," replied Honey, divided between annoyance and a sort of gratification at this evidence that her relations with him seemed to become something of a legend. "Anyway, I ended by getting engaged to him at the beginning of this week."

It would be idle to deny that Honey was now becoming very faintly boastful about her exalted position, and the gasp with which her companion greeted this announcement was flattering in the extreme.

"Then you don't have to worry," the newcomer sighed enviously. "Whatever you did, you wouldn't get into a fight now, I suppose."

You'd be surprised!" replied Honey ironically. "Dr.—I mean John—is a stickler for discipline. I can't imagine that a little thing like being engaged would affect his working manner."

Then she fell to wondering if this really were the case. And, though it is painful to have to record such a thing of our very likeable and conscientious Honey, her attention wandered sadly from her work.

When Dr. Anston finally arrived, she was in the other room. The trembling newcomer fastened his gown and mask for him, and Honey herself did not see him until he actually entered the operating room. By then she was also in the partial disguise of her mask and gown, and there was no question of being able to speak to him personally.

He never even glanced her way. He greeted Sister, nodded to the anesthetist, who was an old friend of his, and gave a curt and comprehensive "Good morning" to the four nurses, including Honey. Then he started to work as usual.

In some extraordinary way, it both amused and excited Honey to know that she was so near him without his even knowing the fact, almost as though she were observing him unseen. He had no reason, of course, to think of her as anything but miles away, and she obviously did not impinge on his consciousness as more than another uniform and another pair of hands.

Part of her was already completely absorbed in the familiar routine of the operating room, but another part of her was quietly enjoying the piquant situation that had arisen. She might have gone on enjoying it all morning. But at this point the doctor cast a keen, critical glance over the instrument trolley, just before giving the sign for the first patient to be wheeled in.

Without even looking up, he said, "Who was responsible for laying up this trolley?"

Honey forgot all about being engaged to him.

"I . . . I was, sir," she stammered.

"Come and look at it."

Honey approached, painfully aware of Sister's angry glance almost boring a hole in her. And she saw that a dreadful, an inconceivable, omission had been made. The very first instrument that Dr. Anston would need was not there.

"I'm sorry, sir." Under her mask, she was scarlet with mortification and naturally kept her head bent. Then, watched by the other nurses, who were sympathetic but profoundly thankful that any victim other than themselves should be offered up on this dreadful occasion, she scurried off to rectify the omission.

Only when this had been done, and it seemed that the scene was at last properly set for the morning's work, did he direct his whole attention on Honey.

"Another time. . . ." he began. Then suddenly he recognized her. "Why, hello, Honey," he exclaimed, taken completely off his guard. "I thought you were still on leave."

It is probable that never before had Sister sustained such a shock. For one thing, she naturally thought Dr. Anston meant "honey" with a small "h," and that he was using this highly unsuitable form of address instead of the more usual "Nurse." In addition, he spoke as though he knew far more about Nurse Milward's non-working activities than was at all desirable.

"Nurse Milward returned early from leave," she said very stiffly, before Honey could find her voice.

"We were short-handed. She was at home, I understand, and not doing anything of special importance."

Quite unexpectedly he laughed at this.

"I wouldn't say that was strictly correct, Sister," he said, obviously in high good humor now. "But at least she settled the important matter early in the week. As a matter of fact, she became engaged to me." .

Then, while Sister, torn between reprimand and congratulation, was trying to think of the right thing to say, he added, "But I think we've mixed private and professional interests quite enough for one morning." And with a brief sign he indicated that he was ready to begin the morning's work.

Mortified as she had been over her early slip, Honey was determined that absolutely nothing would distract her attention again from her work. She ruthlessly thrust Dr. Anston into the background of her mind. And there he remained for the whole of the morning session. Except that, once or twice, when she was watching those strong, beautiful, clever hands, she felt a faint stirring of something like a proprietorial pride in the miraculous things they were able to do.

It was late by the time he had finished, and everyone was glad to relax and think about lunch.

She did not expect him to address her personally again, but, while he was scrubbing up, he glanced over his shoulder at her and said, "Does our evening engagement stand?"

"I . . . . Yes, I think so. I shall be off duty at six."

"Then I'll be at the main entrance with the car at six-thirty. Will that suit you?"

"Yes, yes, certainly," Honey assured him hastily, for she was mortally afraid that this conversation might be overheard by Sister, who would undoub-. tedly regard it as little short of blasphemy that any surgeon should consult the personal convenience of any nurse.

"I have your ring," he continued making matters even worse.

"Have you?" said Honey and fled into the sluice room, where he did not attempt to follow her.

Over her late lunch she had to put up with a good deal of teasing from the other nurses, particularly from those who had been present for the operation, and could not repeat to each other and their friends often enough the particular phrases Dr. Anston had chosen to announce to Sister the news of his engagement.

Although Dr. Anston had finished operating for the day, Honey was busy again that afternoon with one of the other surgeons. Fortunately the session was short, but there was a good deal of clearing up to do later. Thus it was after six before she was able to make her escape.

She was still too new to her changed status to feel anything but nervous at the very thought of keeping any of the surgeons waiting, let alone Dr. Anston. So she rushed off to her room and changed in record time from her uniform to a pretty, flower-printed dress that her father invariably admired; although, in the manner of fathers, he thought it was new every time he commented on it.

At precisely six-thirty, Honey, looking much cooler and calmer than she felt, walked down the steps of the main hospital entrance. As she did so, John Anston got out of his car which was parked nearby, and watched her approach, with that slight, enigmatic smile that always made her wonder just what he was thinking.

"I hope I haven't kept you waiting," said Honey, still rather more nurse than fiancée.

"Not at all," he assured her and, more fiancé than surgeon, coolly bent to kiss her cheek.

Honey flickered her gold-tipped lashes and blushed. And because this annoyed her, she said with unexpected severity, "Was that necessary?"

"I expect so," he replied carelessly. "Anyway, it was very nice." And he held open the door of the car for her.

Honey found nothing whatever to reply to this. And as, on reflection, she guessed that a certain amount of interested observation would have been bestowed upon them in such a public place, she had to admit that he had justice on his side.

They drove out of the hospital grounds in silence—nonplussed on her side but not, she felt sure, in the least on his.

"I thought you might like to have dinner at the Mayflower," said John presently, naming the nearest thing to a roadhouse that the district possessed. "It ought to be pleasant in the gardens on this hot evening."

Honey agreed and tried to look as though going to dine with Dr. Anston were nothing in her young life. But the events of the day pressed too heavily upon her, and presently she burst out, "I'm dreadfully sorry about what happened this morning."

"All right. No harm was done," he told her. "How did it happen, by the way? You're usually so reliable."

A week ago Honey would have been ready to assure anyone that no word of praise from Dr. Anston could cause her even the mildest flutter of gratification. But at this unexpected tribute a warm glow of pleasure spread over her. A sweet, though fugitive, smile lifted the corners of her mouth.

"I'm glad you think so," she said almost shyly. "I really do take the utmost care usually. I suppose perhaps that I was thinking of something else today, just for a moment."

"I suppose you might have been," he conceded with a smile. And then, as though what she had said reminded him of something, he drew the car to a standstill in a pleasant leafy lane.

"Just a moment. You'd better have this before we arrive at the Mayflower," he said. And from his pocket he produced a small jeweler's box.

No one, of course, knew better than Honey that there was no real significance to this moment. No one could be more anxious to insist on the fictitious character of this engagement. And yet, so strong is the power of romantic association, at this moment she suddenly felt a curious tightening of her throat. And when he snapped open the box, to disclose an exquisitely set single-diamond ring, she cried, like any girl to any beloved,

"Oh, how beautiful! How perfectly beautiful!"

"Do you like it?" He smiled.

She nodded wordlessly, though she knew she should really have managed to say something light and amusing, just to show that she was taking this all in the proper spirit of make-believe.

"Shall I put it on for you?"

Again she reminded herself that neither the moment nor the action had any real significance. But when she felt him take her hand lightly, in the strong, clever fingers she knew so well, she felt herself trem- ble unaccountably and, quite absurdly, tears came into her eyes.

"It looks nice on your hand," he observed.

"It would look well on any hand," said Honey, swallowing and managing to speak lightly at last.

"I think not," said John which reduced her to silence once more because she did not quite like to ask him just what he meant by that.

They drove on then, and arrived at the Mayflower, where they were provided with a table in a charmingly terraced garden overlooking the river.

At first she was afraid that it was bound to be a difficult evening of silences and manufactured con- versation. But the excellent food, and possibly the champagne that he declared was proper for an engagement party, made Honey feel more at ease. She found herself not only answering his questions, but volunteering information about herself and her family life.

All the time she was tremendously aware of that slender, sparkling circlet on her left hand. Though she tried not to glance at it too often, it kept on catch- ing her charmed attention at unexpected moments. Once she saw him smiling because she was looking at it, and, blushing, she explained quickly, "It's so beau- tiful that I can't help admiring it. I know it's not really mine, but. . . ."

"It is really yours," stated Dr. Anston.

"Oh no!" She was shocked. "One always gives the ring back when—when. . . ."

"When what?" queried John rather unkindly.

"When an engagement is broken."

"But one never, never," he replied, slightly mimicking her tone, "talks about breaking an engagement on the evening one receives one's ring."

"But in the special circumstances. . . ." she began, half-amused, half-distressed.

"The circumstances of every engagement are special," he declared with conviction. "Enjoy your ring. There's no need to feel self-conscious about it or hide it away."

"I wouldn't dream of hiding it!" Honey declared. "I only wish I could wear it on duty. But I shall certainly wear it on Founder's Day next week; then everyone can see it."

He looked amused and rather pleased, she thought.

"I'd forgotten it was Founder's Day. Next Wednesday, isn't it? I'll have to come down for it."

"Of course. Mother, and possibly my father too, will be there."

"Quite a family party," he observed, but whether or not with pleasure she could not have said.

"How about your sister?" Honey asked feeling that perhaps she should show some spirit of cooperation now that her engagement had been sealed with such a splendid ring. "Do you think she might be in England by then? Because, if so, it might be a good occasion to introduce us to each other and explain the situation."

"I have already explained the situation," said John Anston, who evidently believed in immediate action. "I wrote to her the day after we fixed everything. She should have my letter by now. I'm afraid she is not sailing from New York before Monday or Tuesday, so we won't be able to arrange a meeting on Founder's Day. But we'll find a good opportunity sometime soon."

"Do you think," Honey asked anxiously, "that she

will be upset?" She watched his handsome face relax.

"Upset? About the engagement? Certainly not. She'll be delighted. She has been trying to marry me off for years."

"But she usually chose the candidate, didn't she?" Honey reminded him shrewdly, which appeared to amuse him.

"Don't worry. She'll love you," John said carelessly. The choice of word both touched and disturbed Honey.

"She'd better not love me too much," Honey said soberly, "considering that the whole thing is only going to last a few months."

"True," agreed John. "But as she will spend most of her time in London, there can't be many personal meetings."

"And she really won't be here for more than six months?" Honey suddenly wanted to be reassured on this point, because, in some curious way, the sensation of that ring on her finger imparted a frightening air of permanency to the whole affair.

"She has to be back in the States well before Christmas," he said gravely, though Honey thought there was a gleam of sardonic amusement in his eyes when she drew an involuntary sigh of relief.

"Cheer up," he told her. "Most of the really difficult part is over now. Everyone has been told about the engagement and has accepted it. There now remains only the first meeting with my sister, Deborah. Once that is past, we can settle down to being a conventional engaged couple about whom there is little more to say."

"You don't really suppose the staff at St. Margaret's will ever arrive at that point, do you?" Honey said.

"Why not?"

"Don't you know that, for good or ill, the surgeons in any hospital are a subject of perpetual discussion?"

"Are they?" He looked reflectively amused. "Did you discuss me a great deal before you became engaged to me?"

"Of course. Don't you remember?" she said, with a little touch of malice in return for all the teasing he had enjoyed at her expense.

"Oh! When you called me a monster, you mean?" He laughed, though she thought he was a trifle vexed at the recollection. "Do you still think me a monster, Honey?"

"Do I have to answer that?" Honey said demurely.

"Not if you don't want to," he replied rather disagreeably, "Shall we go now?" and he got up from the table.

She would have liked to tell him she was only teasing him. But there did not seem to be a very good opportunity now. Not, at least, if they were to keep the conversation on a suitably light level.

So she let the subject lapse. They drove home through the early summer night, Honey quietly fingering her ring from time to time, for the sheer pleasure of knowing she had anything so beautiful on her hand.

When he said good night to her, he showed no inclination to kiss her again. Perhaps it was because there was no one about who needed impressing, or perhaps because of what she had said when he greeted her that way.

"I'm going to London for a consultation tomorrow," he told her, "and I doubt if I shall get down again before Wednesday. But I'll try to make it then.

Good night, Honey." His face was near hers, his eyes cool.

She said good night in her turn and then, after the very slightest pause, during which nothing happened, she pulled away her hand quickly and ran up the steps to the big swinging doors.

But, with an inconsistency of which she might well have been ashamed, she thought, as she ran, "I don't know why he didn't kiss me good night. He was quick enough to do it when he greeted me."

CHAPTER FIVE

DURING the next few days, life at St. Margaret's followed a well-worn pattern, as far as Honey was concerned. There were some exciting moments when she displayed her ring to her immediate associates, but otherwise, particularly to her superiors in office, she was just one of the nurses once more.

Meanwhile, preparations and plans for Founder's Day began to take precedence over everything else during off-duty time.

Founder's Day at St. Margaret's was the big day of the year. The Mayor and Mayoress of Forchester always graced the occasion, and all the hospital board attended, in addition to various other local notabilities. By some special favor of Providence, it was nearly always a glorious day, and, as the grounds of the hospital were exceptionally large and beautiful, the whole event tended to take on the character of some immense garden party.

Wards were decorated, not as lavishly as for Christmas, but with a profusion of summer flowers. All the patients who could be moved onto balconies or out of doors took part in the open-air part of proceedings.

Inevitably there were a certain number of speeches, varying in length but usually referred to by their perpetrators as "a few brief words," however inappropriate that description might be in some cases. And of course tea was lavishly served throughout the afternoon, in a big marquee on the center lawn.

Everyone, from the senior surgeon to the most junior nurse, was entitled to have two visitors on this occasion. And all over the green lawns and shady paths were dotted small family groups, each one centered on a student or nurse whose boastful instructiveness was usually in inverse proportion to his or her length of experience.

On previous Founder's Days Honey had been on ward duty. But, as only an emergency operating room was kept open on this day, she was completely free to enjoy her parents' visit on this particular occasion. And when she saw them coming toward her across the lawn, she was not quite sure whether she was more proud to introduce them to St. Margaret's or St. Margaret's to them.

Her mother looked remarkably pretty, and her father sufficiently distinguished to be not only the father of a third-year nurse but the prospective father-in-law of one of the principal surgeons. "Only, of course," thought Honey a little confused, "that doesn't really apply."

"It all looks lovely, darling," her mother said, embracing her affectionately. "Almost a pleasure to be ill in such a setting. Though I suppose," she added candidly, "everyone makes that silly remark, without meaning it any more than I do."

"Is John coming?" asked Mr. Milward, perhaps somewhat overwhelmed by the disproportionate number of females on the scene.

"I hope so," Honey said, kissing him. "But he may be a bit late, as he has to come from London."

"Madame Seroni called to say that she would be coming," observed Mrs. Milward. "She sounded very friendly and was particularly anxious to know if we would be here. She's bringing another member of the family with her. A sister of John's who has just arrived from America."

"A *sister*. . . ."

"Oh, Honey darling," interrupted Mrs. Milward, apparently quite unaware of the expression of consternation on her child's face. "I didn't notice your ring until this moment! Let me look at it. How perfectly beautiful! There's nothing quite like a single diamond, particularly when the setting is so lovely. I remember so well when I was choosing my own. . . ."

"Mother, what did you say about John's sister arriving from America?" interrupted Honey, quite unable to embark on an academic discussion of engagement rings without first having her anxiety on this point satisfied.

"I told you, dear. She has been living in America. . . ."

"Yes, yes, I know that bit. But do you mean she has arrived? She's here?"

"I understand so . . . yes. In fact . . . of course. Because she is coming here this afternoon with Madame Seroni." "But she wasn't supposed to leave America until the day before yesterday. And she was coming by boat."

"Well, I suppose she changed her mind, my dear. Why not?" inquired Mrs. Milward, to whom a change of mind quite often commended itself.

"Then she won't have seen John. Unless she saw him as she came through London."

"No, she didn't come through London," Mrs. Milward said. "I remember now. Madame Seroni explained that her plane had been diverted for some reason. Engine trouble or something of the sort. And so she came on here, as she meant to spend a few days with Madame Seroni in any case."

"So that he won't have had time to . . . to explain about our engagement?"

"Never mind, darling. I'm sure Madame Seroni has explained everything beautifully, so what's the difference?" asked her mother mildly.

"I just thought it would be better. . . ."

Honey's voice trailed away. She tried to pull herself together and believe that there was no reason to panic.

After all, she told herself, there was no need to feel so bereft and unprotected, just because Dr. Anston was not there to help her tackle this particular interview. He was not so important in every phase of her life, surely?

But even as she assured herself of this, her mother exclaimed in a pleased tone, "Here they are!"

And, with an unaccountable sinking of her heart, Honey saw the impressive figure of Madame Seroni approaching her. Beside her, was a tall elegant woman who must, she supposed, be Dr. Anston's sister.

With a gracious little wave of her hand, usually reserved for much larger audiences, Madame Seroni bore down upon the Milwards like a handsome yacht in full sail. There was a flurry of introductions, and Honey found her hand taken in firm, cool fingers that had a touch of the same purposeful strength as John's, and a pleasant voice said, "So this is Honey?"

"We . . . didn't expect you quite so soon," Honey explained shyly. "Dr. An—John thought you would be coming by boat."

"That was the original arrangement. But there have been a lot of last-minute changes." Deborah Naylor smiled at Honey in a way that reminded one of her brother. "I'm staying here for only a month, after all. . . ."

"A month!" For some quite inexplicable reason, Honey was aghast, instead of profoundly relieved, as she should have been.

"Yes. Then I'm returning to the States for a few weeks, just to settle up our affairs there," John's sister went on. "My husband has been offered a very good position in the firm's London office, and so we're returning home for good."

"For . . . for good?" stammered Honey, and a sudden chill crept down her spine.

"Yes. It's all quite unexpected, of course. But doubly welcome now that John is getting married. I should have simply hated missing all the fun. Now I shall be in on it all," declared Deborah Naylor warmly.

"I do understand!" exclaimed Mrs. Milward, visibly moved by this evidence of interest in her daughter's affairs. "Isn't it splendid, Honey dear?"

"Splendid," echoed Honey dear, in a hollow voice. And, almost before her eyes, as it were, her pretended engagement to Dr. Anston began to take on inescapable reality.

Weddings, so she had been assured, were the breath of life to Deborah Naylor, and she could well believe it. For already this charming, determined, efficient creature obviously saw herself steering things to a satisfactory conclusion, in a general atmosphere of confetti and orange blossom.

It was greatly to Honey's social credit that, during

the whole of that first hour with Deborah, she some-how contrived to conceal the fact that she was com-pletely horrified by the prospect of her returning to live in England.

"Such a delightful coincidence that it should be just now that you're returning to live here," Mrs. Milward said sincerely.

And Honey actually managed to murmur, "Yes, indeed!" with a shy but completely convincing smile.

"I can't tell you how much I've wanted to see John happily married," Deborah declared, with a degree of feeling that obviously commended itself to Mrs. Mil-ward but secretly depressed Honey.

"He's a darling, you know," Deborah went on, "and so clever, but just a bit too reserved and with-drawn. Though I don't expect you know that side of him, Honey," she added with a good-humored laugh.

Honey said with some feeling that, on the contrary, she knew exactly what Deborah meant.

"Well, men get like that, I guess, when they're wrapped up in their work or their hobby," Dr. Anston's sister continued reflectively. "And to John his surgery is both."

"We heard him speak about his work in a lecture," Mrs. Milward hastened to explain. "And we were enormously impressed by his attitude toward it. He was very amusing and charming, but one felt—" she dropped her voice impressively—"that he is a dedi-cated person."

"Yes, indeed." Deborah seemed to like the phrase. "But that's all the more reason for his needing a wife in the background. A pretty, charming, intelligent wife like you, Honey. She smiled so warmly and approvingly that Honey felt like a dreadful fraud.

"Above all, he needs someone who can appreciate and understand his work. That's why this match is ideal. Really, it will be the happiest day of my life when I see you two married," she finished, with what was obviously some exaggeration, but a genuinely felt emotion.

"Yes," said Honey, in answer to all this. And then, because the one monosyllable seemed so ungracious and inadequate, she felt bound to add, though blushing for her falseness, "It will naturally be the happiest day of my life too."

The others all smiled sympathetically, evidently mistaking the cause of the blush. Even her father looked somewhat moved, while Madame Seroni said, with some emotion, that this would be an occasion when she would feel justified in emerging from semi-retirement, and that she hoped to sing at Honey's wedding.

"Oh, Madame Seroni!" exclaimed Mrs. Milward, obviously remembering those command performances of *The Messiah* and thinking delightedly of her child's wedding in the same category. And although she was, of course, much too polite to say that would be one over Miss Emms, to Honey at least it was patent that this unworthy thought was passing through her mother's mind.

It was frightening to think how many disappointments were in store for people she loved or liked. But still more frightening was the curious conviction that when Deborah Naylor set her heart on anything it almost invariably came to pass.

"I only have to say 'no,'" Honey kept on telling herself. "I only have to be firm about breaking off the engagement." But she glanced at the pleasant, strong-featured face of Dr. Anston's sister and wondered how one could match such firmness.

They all strolled about the sunlit grounds for a while. The older ladies at any rate were more interested in the delightful discussion of personal matters than in anything to do with the hospital or its founder. Then Honey suggested that they should come in to see some of the wards, and Deborah said she would at any rate like to see where her brother worked.

So Honey took them all along to the operating room, which looked oddly unfamiliar in its silent and deserted condition. In spite of Madame Seroni's declaration that it gave her the creeps, they all seemed anxious to hear whatever Honey had to tell them. She was in the middle of an impromptu lecture on operating routines when Dr. Anston arrived.

"John!" His sister flung her arms around him and greeted him with an affectionate warmth that he obviously returned. For a few minutes there was nothing but a spate of explanations.

John, like Honey a little while earlier, emerged from the torrent of words with one fact perfectly clear.

"You say," his voice was studiedly calm and deliberate, "that you and Ronald are returning here to live."

"Yes, Yes! I'm here for a month." His sister was only too willing to recapitulate her happy tale. "Then I return to the States to settle up everything. It shouldn't take longer than five or six weeks, and then, back home to England for good. And to think that it's all so well timed, that I shall be here for all the wedding preparations, and the actual ceremony! It's hardly to be believed." She beamed happily at them.

"Hardly to be believed," agreed John, meeting Honey's gaze without flinching.

"I'm so happy about it all," Deborah exclaimed, with so much good feeling that everyone had to smile sympathetically. "And dear Honey says, of course, that it will be the happiest day of her life."

"Did dear Honey really say that?" John looked at Honey with something like amused congratulation. For a moment his gray eyes warmed and sparkled in a way she would not have thought possible.

"Naturally," said Honey demurely.

To which Dr. Anston merely murmured, "Dear girl!" and drew her arm through his. Then, turning to the others, he asked, "Has Honey been doing the honors in the operating room?"

"Very inadequately, darling," said Honey, feeling he deserved that, after involving her in such a dilemma.

But he took the endearment in his stride, sarcastic though he must have known it to be, and, lightly kissing the side of her cheek, he said, "I'm sure you did it beautifully. But this is all too much of a busman's holiday. Shall we go and have tea now?" This suggestion commended itself to all, and a move was made in the direction of the grounds and the big marquee.

Even Deborah realized that Honey and her devoted fiancé would naturally wish to have a few precious minutes together. So, hard though it was not to appropriate her brother at this moment, she joined the others and walked on ahead, leaving the happy couple to follow more slowly.

Thus it was that Honey was able to say in a small, grim voice, "And where do we go from here?"

"I'm sorry. It's a most unexpected complication," John conceded, a little too carelessly she thought. "But there's no need to panic."

"I'm not panicking," said Honey, who had at least been very near it at one point. "I just want you to know that I'm furious, and that I think I must have been stark staring mad ever to take this thing on and expect you to steer me clear of disaster."

"My charming and furious Honey," he said with that very slight but personal smile that always reassured the most nervous of his patients, "are you trying to tell me that you've lost faith in my power to deal with the situation?"

"I . . . I . . . not exactly," said Honey, much more pacifically, because, when he spoke like that, Dr. Anston seemed so completely capable of dealing with any situation. "It's just that it makes me nervous when your sister so openly rejoices in the wedding details, and your aunt says graciously that she'll sing an anthem or something. I can see my mother planning out my trousseau almost before my eyes. The whole thing is beginning to seem so real that I can almost smell the orange-blossom and hear the bells ring."

"I'm so sorry. It does sound real, put like that," agreed John. But, though his words were sympathetic, he laughed rather heartlessly.

"I've had to remind myself deliberately, for most of the past hour, that the whole thing is a masquerade and simply cannot turn into the real thing," Honey said severely.

"You'd hate it so much, of course, if it did turn into the real thing, wouldn't you?" Dr. Anston returned lightly.

"I don't think," said Honey, drawing her arm away,

"that's even a good joke." She spoke reproachfully.

"No," he agreed, rubbing his chin reflectively. "I think perhaps you're right. It wasn't even a good joke."

And then his sister, unable to spare him any longer, even to the most devoted of fiancées, turned and waited for them to come up with her.

"John, dear," she said, "there's so much to discuss that I don't even know where to begin." Then she proceeded to make a very handsome beginning. By the time they reached the marquee, Honey was no longer called on to do more than smile, look happy and add an occasional enthusiastic assent to Deborah Naylor's eager planning.

With a sort of abandoned recklessness Honey agreed to everything that his sister proposed. In some obscure way, she managed to hold Dr. Anston responsible for this. After all, if she were not to oppose anyone on the vital issue of the wedding itself, if she were not to be allowed to say that the whole thing was one gigantic mistake and fraud, then it seemed somewhat pointless to argue the toss over the number of bridesmaids, or the number of guests, or the place for the ceremony and reception.

"A hospital wedding would be lovely," Deborah Naylor declared. "Nurses forming a guard of honor, patients waving from the windows and all that sort of thing." She made a vague but comprehensive gesture that seemed to sketch in the scene before their eyes.

Mrs. Milward, however, had other ideas.

"But there's nothing more beautiful and touching than a village wedding," she countered quickly. "And we have such a lovely village church, and the vicar christened Honey...." Tears filled her eyes at this moving recollection, although, in point of fact, Honey had disgraced them all on that occasion by howling throughout the ceremony. "I don't think Honey would want to be married anywhere else. Would you darling?"

"And then one must think of Miss Emms and the other institute members," put in Honey's father slyly, thus saving her from the necessity of making an immediate decision.

"Exactly!" Mrs. Milward took this up in all earnestness. "They were all so thrilled with John when he came to speak to them. They feel that in some way he almost belongs to them. And then, of course, most of them have known Honey since she was a little girl."

And, at the thought of this beautiful continuity of village interest, Mrs. Milward really did have to touch her handkerchief to her eyes.

"Yes, I do see. . . . Oh really, I see your point absolutely," Deborah conceded with immediate generosity. At which the two ladies fell into an enjoyable discussion about floral decorations, undeterred by the fact that the wedding date had not yet been fixed, and that it was therefore impossible to say what flowers would be available.

"And what do you say to all this?" inquired Dr. Anston softly of Honey. "Do you vote for me to lead you to the village altar, or does the idea of the hospital chapel seem more attractive?"

Honey shot him an angry glance from under her gold-tipped lashes, and only just bit back an explosive, "Neither, thank you, at any price!"

For she thought that, having involved her in this situation, he might at least have had the grace to refrain from teasing her about it. It was surely enough that her mother and his sister must discuss it in all its details, without his inviting her, quite gratuitously, to join in the discussion.

So, except for that one angry, but beautiful, glance at him, she pretended not to hear him and turned instead to talk to her father.

This was a very welcome diversion, since Madame Seroni, apropos her own part in the ceremony, was putting Mr. Milward through his paces on the subject of English church music and finding him sadly wanting.

For a few minutes Honey managed to talk to her father about what she secretly characterized to herself as "sane subjects." But then the conversation became general once more, and she heard her mother say, "It's so refreshing to find a sister so devotedly interested in her brother's affairs. I'm sure we are all going to enjoy this wedding even more for having you with us, Mrs. Naylor."

Deborah Naylor said that was very sweet of Mrs. Milward. But Dr. Anston grinned sardonically and remarked, "My sister is an inveterate match-maker, Mrs. Milward. She has been finding prospective wives for me ever since I was old enough to refuse them. Why, she even had one who was coming over on the boat with her. Isn't that right, Deborah?"

"Oh, well. . . ." Deborah laughed a little self-consciously and even had the grace to blush slightly, though she was evidently not seriously put out by her brother's teasing.

"So, you see, I had to get engaged to Honey, in sheer self-defense," declared Dr. Anston, taking what Honey considered to be an almost fiendish pleasure in giving the truth every appearance of an amusing lie. She couldn't understand why he did this.

"Millicent wouldn't really have done," his sister admitted thoughtfully. "I realize that now I've seen Honey."

And she smiled so approvingly at Honey that Honey's parents could not hide their gratification and made only the feeblest attempt to a graceful appearance of finding Deborah's praise a little excessive.

This atmosphere of harmony persisted throughout tea. But, before the party split up to go their separate ways, Deborah insisted that another important decision must be taken.

"You must come to London, my dear," she assured Honey, "and stay with me at the Gloria. Your mother too, of course. When can you have a few days' leave?"

"Leave? Oh, I have no leave left," Honey declared in panic.

"Yes, you have, darling," her mother reminded her. "You must have at least three days' leave owing to you, after going back on duty to oblige Matron. Don't you remember?"

Reluctantly, Honey remembered.

"But we're terribly busy," she insisted anxiously. "I think it would be impossible—"

"I'm sure it could be managed," interposed Dr. Anston smoothly, and Honey restrained with difficulty a desire to kick his ankle under the table.

"What makes you think that?" she inquired a little coldly.

"Things can always be arranged if one wants them sufficiently," he said coolly.

"You tell that to Sister!"

"I will," said Dr. Anston almost carelessly, and Honey was reduced to silence.

Deborah was delighted.

"John and I," already speaking for her brother in his matrimonial affairs, "naturally want you to meet some of our friends, Honey dear. And it isn't too soon to think about trousseau shopping either. Dear me! What fun this is all going to be!"

Mrs. Milward cordially echoed this sentiment and was obviously so pleased at the idea of a few days' shopping and festivity in London that Honey felt it was mean of her to want to veto the entire arrangement.

Besides, since she was the chief figure in the drama, she supposed she should at least try to match the enthusiasm of the others. And presently, to her mingled chagrin and astonishment, she found herself expressing something like joy at the prospect of being more and more deeply involved in complications.

By the time she said goodbye to her parents and the other two ladies, at the hospital gates, the matter was as good as settled in principle. Honey and her mother were to go to London and stay with Deborah at the Gloria, just as soon as a few days' leave became available.

CHAPTER SIX

WHEN Madame Seroni's handsome Rolls-Royce and Mr. Milward's somewhat shabbier car had driven away, Honey and John turned and strolled back toward the hospital in silence.

Honey felt almost too vexed and distressed to say anything, and he seemed to be calmly unaware of the fact that apologies and explanations were called for. Indeed, when he did finally·speak, all he said was, "How soon do you expect to have your leave?"

Honey glanced at him.

"Meadows came back yesterday," she admitted reluctantly, "and two of the others are expected by the weekend. I suppose I could have it next week . . . if I wanted it."

"But don't you?" He sounded no more than mildly surprised at the idea that someone should be willing to sacrifice several days of their leave.

Honey took a deep breath and counted to ten.

"Don't you think," she said, in a dangerously quiet voice, "that it would be wiser for me to pretend that I couldn't get away during the month your sister is here?"

"No," he said, without elaboration.

"But, Dr. Anston, if Mother and I go to London and I'm shown around to your friends as your fiancée, and there is trousseau buying and goodness knows what else, the whole thing will get completely out of hand. You must see that!" Honey felt overwhelmed.

"On the contrary," he assured her. "Opposition only stimulates Deborah. If we have no arguments and appear to do exactly what she proposes, everything will go on quite smoothly and uneventfully. Then, when she has returned to the States, we can rearrange things to suit ourselves."

"But she's returning there only for about a month or six weeks," Honey reminded him.

"That's long enough to break any engagement," declared John carelessly. And, for some perverse reason she could not have explained, Honey felt furious with him for speaking of their engagement in that slighting way.

"Have you thought," she asked coldly, "how unpleasant my position here in the hospital is going to be, when the news of the broken engagement leaks out?"

"My dear, you'll be the heroine of the place," he retorted, with what she thought ill-timed humor. "You will be doing the jilting, remember."

"I don't *want* to be doing any jilting!" exclaimed Honey angrily. "It's . . . it's not my idea of nice behavior at all."

"But think of it," he urged her teasingly. "You will not only appear as the girl who tamed the monster to the point of an engagement. You will even have rejected him as not good enough, on further consideration."

"Dr. Anston, that isn't funny." Honey's voice actually trembled. "I'm not that type of girl at all. This ridiculous business started as a silly kind of masquerade, I know, but at least it was designed to help you out of what you represented as a dilemma. I don't want to be cast in the role of some sort of heartless and cynical flirt. I'm very unhappy about my position as it is. And you're not being particularly k-kind about it."

She bit her lip hard, because excitement and nervousness were bringing her very near tears.

"My dear Honey," his voice altered, and he drew her arm through his in a way that was curiously consoling and steadying, "I apologize. Tell me what you really want me to do, in the changed circumstances, and I'll do it."

"I don't really know what to suggest," Honey said unhappily.

"Do you want to go on with the engagement indefinitely?"

"No. Of course not!"

"No, no. I meant, rather, for the length of time originally planned," Dr. Anston explained soothingly. "That would bring you to the end of your training here, at St. Margaret's. Then you could leave, as you always intended, still as my fiancée, and start at a new hospital or in private nursing without any embarrassing restrictions. That was the original idea, if you remember."

"But—" Honey glanced anxiously from under her gold-tipped lashes, "—that means months as your fiancée, with Deborah and my mother pressing all the time for us to fix the date of the wedding and make all the preparations."

"Yes," he agreed, "I'm afraid it does. But can't you cope with that? It's only a question of keeping your own counsel and more or less ignoring what is happening around you."

"But, Dr. Anston—" she was aghast at so clear a

description of the position, "—I couldn't live like that! *You* may be able to, but I can't. I'm part of an intimate and loving home circle. I couldn't go home on weekends and have my mother making happy arrangements and holding long-distance phone calls with Deborah, while I smiled and pretended and knew all the time that the whole thing was one gigantic fraud."

"You would have had to do something of the sort under the original plan," he reminded her.

"Oh no! Left to myself, I could have kept everything on a much quieter and slower basis. Now that your sister has invaded my home scene and swept my mother into her whirl of planning, it's all taken on quite a different complexion."

"But that too was a possibility under the original plan," he said. "Hadn't you reckoned with it?"

For a long moment Honey was silent. Then, with a lone tear splashing onto each cheek, she said unsteadily, "I guess—I'm not—the right sort of girl for this job."

"I guess," he agreed thoughtfully, "you're not." And, unexpectedly, he bent his head and softly kissed the side of her cheek. "I'm sorry. The mistake was mine. I admit I had quite a lot of wrong ideas about you, Honey, before I got to know you better."

"I had—a few—about you," Honey admitted generously.

He laughed at that, but said in a businesslike tone, "Well then, let's settle this affair on a friendly basis. It's simply a question of deciding the best point at which to break the engagement. We could, of course, do it at once, and thereby cut our way through all complications."

But Honey thought this would be too sensational.

"The engagement is still a nine days' wonder in the hospital," she said soberly. "To break it at this point would make us both look too frivolous and idiotic for words. I think we'd better go on until your sister returns to the States. But *please* play the whole thing down as much as possible, will you? And I will do the same at home."

"I'll do my best." John promised gravely, and with such friendly docility that somehow Honey suddenly remembered that this was, after all, the most distinguished surgeon at St. Margaret's who was taking her orders.

"And I will go to London, if you think that's best," she said, feeling that some concession on her part was called for.

"I really do," he assured her. "Deborah opposed is capable of almost anything. She adores removing obstacles. If we appear to go on quietly following her plans there will be no need for argument or awkward discussion. Then when she has left England once more, you and I can break things up as discreetly and unembarrassingly as possible."

"There'll be a whole lot of explanations due when she returns," Honey could not help reminding him.

"But those, my dear Honey, will be my affair," he replied calmly. "You need not know anything about them. You need not even see Deborah again unless you wish."

"I suppose not," agreed Honey and was immediately assailed by a sort of melancholy curiosity. She would be sorry to be so far removed from Dr. Anston's affairs that she must not even inquire about anything so vitally interesting to herself.

"Then it's settled?" They had reached the side entrance to the nurses' residence by now, and he paused, smiling down at her from his considerable height.

"Yes. It's settled. I'll take my leave toward the end of next week, if I can, and Mother and I will go to London."

"Good girl."

"You'll make a point of being there, won't you?" she exclaimed, suddenly frightened at the idea of possibly being abandoned to the busy plans of her mother and Deborah, not to mention a host of unknown Anston friends.

"Of course," he promised soothingly. "That's the whole purpose of the trip, you know, that you and I should be seen together. Don't worry. I'll look after you."

And so powerful was the spell of his smiling, half-mocking assurance that Honey went away thinking almost entirely of his final words, and hardly at all about the further complication to which she had now committed herself.

Several of her fellow nurses had, of course, seen her in company with her parents and Dr. Anston. However much they might have been taken up with their own families and visitors, they had spared more than a glance—and probably more than a word of explanation—for the nurse who was to marry their most famous surgeon.

"You looked rather good together, Milward," someone said.

And, "It was plain for anyone to see how devoted he is," added the sentimental Morgan. "Who were the two ladies with him and your parents?"

Honey explained about Madame Seroni and Dr. Anston's sister, and everyone seemed to think they were a distinct addition to the situation.

"I heard one of them call you 'dear,'" remarked Peters, who had somehow got near enough in the tea tent to pick up this interesting detail. "Would that be the sister? And how does she like the match?"

With difficulty Honey kept herself from saying, "All too well."

"She seems very happy about it," Honey explained sedately. And then, perhaps to satisfy Peters's thirst for knowledge, or perhaps because the subject had a certain strange fascination for herself, she added, "Mother and I are going to London next week, if I can get my few days' leave then. We're to stay at the Gloria as Mrs. Naylor's guests."

Peters whistled at this, for the Gloria, of course, is known to all as that palace of a hotel where one may sit in the immense lounge and expect to see anyone, from an archbishop to a prima donna, pass by.

"Lucky you!" sighed Morgan. "My! How your life has changed in the past few weeks, Milward."

Honey said with feeling that indeed it had. And then, fortunately, it was time for most of them to go on duty. During the next few days Honey tried to accustom herself to the fresh development in her life. She had, without too much difficulty, accepted the idea of a more or less theoretical engagement to Dr. Anston. She had even become used to having her fellow nurses look at her a little differently because of it. But now she was to emerge onto a much wider stage, as it were, and play her part before a much more exacting audience.

Dr. Anston had said he would look after her and, in

a way, she was sure he would. That had seemed all right on the day of the garden party. But now, the more she thought about that trip to London, the more it seemed to her that some fearful new development was almost bound to arise.

The gesture appeared to her at this point to have been altogether too bold, and she wished she could recall it. But this would be impossible without seeming to let Dr. Anston down.

She saw little of him during this time, except in the operating room. And there, even now, he was the impersonal, remote Dr. Anston, to be treated as the god of his particular domain and not at all as a fiancé to whom one could take one's foolish fears and objections.

Before he himself returned to London, however, he did contrive to see her for a few minutes' private conversation, in between spells of duty.

"I won't be down here at all in the first half of next week, Honey," he explained. "Let me know when you expect to be in London, won't you?"

"It's already settled," she told him. "I shall come off duty on Wednesday at lunchtime, and Mother will pick me up here. That means we shall be in London some time on Wednesday evening. Mother has written to your . . . to Deborah to tell her."

"Fine. Which train will you take? I'll meet you at the other end."

But Honey said that there was too much doubt about the actual hour of her release. It would be better for them to go straight to the Gloria on their arrival, and then either they or Deborah would telephone him from there.

"Very well. Look after yourself and don't be nervous about the visit. Nothing dreadful is going to happen," he assured her lightheartedly. "All you have to do is to relax, and be ready to enjoy a certain amount of gaiety without worrying too much about the situation that has prompted it."

Then he kissed her lightly, although there was no one in sight who needed to be impressed with the authenticity of their relationship. He went away, leaving Honey with the conviction that she now knew exactly how it was that he managed to make his patients believe they had nothing to fear once they were in his hands.

This feeling persisted, though with diminishing intensity, until the day of her departure for London.

In spite of any inner misgivings, Honey could not, of course, feel anything but thrilled and excited when she finally emerged from the residence into the bright sunshine of a perfect summer's day, to find both her parents waiting for her in the family car.

"Daddy managed to get away from the office for an hour or two, so he's driving us to the junction," Mrs. Milward explained as she kissed her daughter. "That makes it possible for us to catch the earlier train."

Honey beamed at her father and climbed into the back of the car. At which her mother turned sideways and studied her in a contented way.

"That particular shade of yellow is extraordinarily becoming, Honey dear," she said reflectively. "I think you should have ivory, or even perhaps parchment color for your wedding dress. Not dead white. Certainly not dead white. What do you think, James?"

Mr. Milward said he was sure Honey would look pretty in anything. A maddening statement that was partly due to parental prejudice and partly to a cowardly desire to avoid committing himself to an opinion his wife would almost certainly challenge.

"Your mother has the checkbook, Honey," he explained, with the air of being a willing victim on the altar of his womenfolk's extravagance. "And she has permission to use it to the limit. So see that you get what you really want."

"Oh, Daddy!" Honey leaned forward and patted his shoulder almost tearfully, for she was overcome by a confused feeling that she was little better than someone who stole her poor old parents' savings in order to advance a career of deceit. "I . . . I don't expect I shall want anything much on this trip. It's too early yet to do much shopping.".

"Your mother seems to think otherwise," replied Mr. Milward, who, like most husbands and fathers, preferred to refer to his wife as "your mother" whenever strictly feminine interests were under discussion.

"Well, we'll see," declared Mrs. Milward, with an air of brisk cheerfulness. And then they drove the rest of the way to the junction, with Honey sitting back and hoping that her mother and Deborah Naylor between them would not reduce her father to actual penury.

After affectionate goodbyes at the station, Honey felt still less inclined to spend her father's money under false pretenses. But, comfortably installed with Honey in an otherwise empty compartment, Mrs. Milward launched into contented planning for a shopping spree, on a scale that greatly alarmed Honey.

"But, Mother," she repeated anxiously, "I don't want to do much shopping on this trip. It's much too early, as I said to Daddy."

"Not if you're going to be married in October, my

dear," was the almost absent reply her mother made.

"But who says I am going to be married in October?" Honey looked taken aback.

"It's the obvious choice, isn't it? You aren't planning on a winter wedding, surely?"

"No, indeed," said Honey emphatically. For winter loomed menacingly near when her mother put it like that.

"And I can't imagine that either of you would want to wait until next spring?"

"We might," Honey set her soft mouth in an unexpectedly obstinate line. "There's no need to rush things like this, Mother."

"Darling, no one is trying to *rush* you at all!" Mrs. Milward sounded rather indignant at the choice of word. "But, when two people are as sure of their feelings as you and John are. . . ."

Where did Mother get that idea? thought Honey, annoyed.

". . . there isn't any need to wait too long. I can't say that I see the point of your going on wearing yourself out at the hospital, when you are really going to marry John."

"I'm not wearing myself out," protested Honey indignantly, for none of us like to be described in this somewhat dreary phrase. "But I naturally want to complete my training," she added, snatching hastily at this form of protection.

"Oh, but, Honey—why?"

"Because I don't believe in leaving things unfinished," Honey said, with increased firmness. "And, besides, if you're a trained nurse, you always have a profession at your fingertips and a way of earning a living if—if anything happens."

"If what happens?"

"Oh, just anything," Honey said feebly.

"I don't understand you. As John's wife, you'll hardly need a profession, or a way of earning a living."

"One never knows," stated Honey. At that her mother opened her eyes wide in astonishment—perhaps understandably since the only contingencies which Honey could possibly be referring to were widowhood or separation. Neither of them were very appropriate subjects on which to linger when going to choose one's trousseau.

"Well, my dear, of course it's for you to decide," conceded Mrs. Milward, evidently abandoning the idea of the October wedding with regret. "But talk things over with John, and remember there are his wishes to be consulted too. He doesn't strike me as at all the kind of man who would want to postpone his wedding for the sake of nursing certificates, once he had found the girl of his heart."

This romantic view of Dr. Anston faintly intrigued Honey, and she spent some time after that looking out of the window of the train and wondering just what Dr. Anston would be like if he really were in love with someone.

It was still no more than late afternoon when they arrived in London. Warm sunshine was alternating with cool shade in the park, as they drove to the Gloria.

Here, rooms were engaged for them next to Mrs. Naylor's suite, and the desk clerk informed them that Mrs. Naylor herself was in the lounge, having tea with a friend, if they wished to speak to her before going to their rooms.

"Yes, I think we will," Mrs. Milward said. Even as she turned to look for Deborah, she came hurrying toward them with almost literally open arms.

"My dears, I'm so glad to see you!" This was so palpably true that Honey had another moment of acute remorse for the falseness of her position. "Come and join us for tea."

Mrs. Milward said they would not interrupt a tête-à-tête between friends. But Deborah exclaimed, "Nonsense! Millicent Eldon arrived from New York only a few days ago, and she's longing to meet you. You'll like her immensely."

Like most of us on being assured of such a state of affairs, Honey decided perversely that she would not. And, in any case, the name struck an uneasy chord in her memory. But she naturally bowed to necessity and followed her mother and Deborah Naylor across the lounge.

As she did so, she remembered. Millicent was the name of the girl Deborah had once thought of as such a suitable wife for Dr. Anston.

This fact immediately imparted to her a distinct, though inexplicably unwelcome, significance. Honey felt an odd resentment stirring in her heart as Millicent Eldon's cool fingers touched hers, and she realized that this was quite one of the most beautiful girls she had ever seen.

Not that "girl" was a word one would instinctively apply to Millicent Eldon. She was probably no more than 26 or 27, but her poise and charming air of sophisticated elegance were attributes that one usually associated with someone a good deal older.

She was perfectly agreeable to Honey, while Mrs. Milward and Deborah exchanged a few words about the evening's arrangements. But suddenly Honey felt young and extraordinarily insecure.

Millicent Eldon intimidated her far more than the palatial surroundings of the Gloria could do, and she heard her usual easy flow of friendly talk dry up to a trickle of conventional and uninspiring platitudes.

"John told me quite a lot about you," the other girl said carelessly. And immediately Honey found herself wondering just what he had said about her, and how this girl had managed to get on such terms of intimacy with him in a matter of a few days.

To her annoyance, she could think of nothing to say but "Did he?" And she knew, almost as though it had been put into words, that Millicent Eldon was wondering what on earth the brilliant John Anston had seen in this inarticulate young nobody.

Fortunately, as soon as tea was over, Honey and her mother were wafted up to their own rooms on the second floor, while Deborah undertook to telephone her brother and let him know that their visitors had arrived somewhat sooner than they had expected.

Honey and her mother discovered that they had very pleasant rooms, with a communicating door, overlooking the park. And, as soon as they were left alone, Mrs. Milward came into Honey's room and said, "So *that* was the girl Deborah thought of for John's wife. What an extraordinary idea!"

"Oh, Mother, why? She's very good-looking and charming," Honey felt bound to point out. Though, in reality, her mother's disparaging air did much for her own *amour propre*.

"But she isn't at all John's type. I'm not surprised that he chose you in preference."

"Not exactly in preference," Honey reminded her

mother with a smile. "He hadn't seen her when he—chose me."

"Then he must have congratulated himself when he did," retorted Mrs. Milward complacently. "She has been here a day or two now so he has had time to see what a lucky escape he has had."

"I don't expect he thinks of it that way at all." Honey spoke with an obstinacy that she could not quite explain even to herself. "And anyway, Mother dear, I don't know how you can be quite so sure about John's taste. You don't really know him all that well, do you?"

"But *you're* his taste, darling!" Her mother looked surprised. "And you and this girl could hardly be more different."

"That's true, of course," Honey agreed soberly.

"Not that I'm criticizing her," said Mrs. Milward somewhat belatedly and not especially truthfully. "I'm sure she is a very charming creature and would make an excellent wife for a certain type of man. But not John."

Honey had no answer to this. Mostly because the oddly depressing thought had come to her that possibly Millicent Eldon *would* make an excellent wife for a busy and famous surgeon. She would be admirable as a hostess, a genuine social asset to any man, and she would be quite unruffled by any unusual circumstance that might arise.

Possibly her silence struck her mother as not entirely happy, because Mrs. Milward said cheerfully, after a moment, "Well, this is quite an academic discussion, in any case, isn't it? Dear John has given us the clearest proof of his taste, in asking you to marry him. And it isn't only maternal prejudice that makes me think his taste is excellent! You *are* lovely, you know."

And, laughing a little, she went back into her own room and began to unpack. For a few minutes longer Honey stood by the window, looking out across the park and wondering, though without her mother's pleasant peace of mind, just what Dr. Anston's taste really was.

Soon she too began to unpack. But she had not got very far with this when the telephone rang, and one of the clerks at the reception desk informed her that Dr. Anston was waiting downstairs and would be happy to see her whenever she was ready.

"Tell him I won't be more than ten minutes," Honey said quickly, and then she went to tell her mother that John was waiting for them.

"Not for us, darling," said her mother indulgently. "Just for you, I imagine. I'm sure he can wait a little longer before seeing me. You go down to him. I'll finish the unpacking. And wear your brown dress, Honey. It does things for you."

So, sustained by the leaf-brown cocktail dress that "did things for her," and some attractive chunky gold costume jewelry that Miss Emms had once character-ized as too daring, Honey went away to join Dr. Anston.

It was the time of evening when there was a great deal of coming and going, and even the elevators at the Gloria were not quite equal to the demand. For some minutes Honey stood there, watching crowded elevators pass her by. Then, recalling that she had only two flights of stairs to descend, she went down by the wide, curving staircase, that led straight into the huge, thickly carpeted lounge.

On the last few steps she paused, surveying the crowded scene, with a pleasure only tinged with nervousness. Deborah was nowhere in sight, and for a moment she could not pick out Dr. Anston either.

And then she saw him standing not so very far away from the foot of the staircase.

He should, of course, have been looking eagerly for her arrival, either from one of the elevators, or from the stairs. But he was doing nothing of the sort.

Instead, he was standing there, laughing down rather challengingly at Millicent Eldon. And, even as Honey watched, with suddenly widened eyes, she saw Millicent lean forward and pick an imaginary thread from the lapel of Dr. Anston's dinner jacket; with a teasing, proprietorial little gesture used only between people who are very, very good friends.

CHAPTER SEVEN

As Honey stood there on the great main staircase of the Gloria, watching this intimate little scene between Millicent Eldon and Dr. Anston, she was overwhelmed by immeasurable surprise. Not because Millicent was being charmingly provocative and flirtatious. Not even because Dr. Anston was accepting her overtures with apparent pleasure. But because the sight of all this moved her to the most furious and ungovernable dismay.

How dared this unknown girl touch her Dr. Anston in that casual and possessive manner! And how dared he allow her to do so anyway! Surely this was a moment when he should have taken a step backward and bestowed on her the kind of icy glance with which he had frozen Honey herself whenever he considered she had erred or presumed.

Honey had not felt so angry and outraged for years—not since the little girl next door had walked off with her doll's carriage and calmly assumed ownership. Indeed, in some curious way, the occasions were not dissimilar. Summary justice had been dealt out over the doll's carriage in the shape of a good tug at the offender's hair. And, again to her shocked surprise, Honey realized that something in her, primitive and hitherto unsuspected, clamored for similar treatment of this incident.

She controlled herself, however, summoned a friendly smile to her faintly unsteady lips, and descended the last few stairs. But, even then, she remained unnoticed, and she had to go right up to Dr. Anston and say, "Hello, John," in a smaller voice than she had intended, before he realized that she was there.

She had to admit that he then made handsome amends for his previous neglect for, putting his arm around her, he drew her quite close against him and said, "Why, darling! I didn't notice you coming, although I watched the elevators. Where did you spring from?"

She wanted to say that she had been standing on the stairway for the past five minutes and that he had been watching Millicent Eldon's antics, not the elevators. But, as the first statement would have been inaccurate and the second impolitic, she somehow suppressed both and merely said that she had come down by the stairs.

He kissed her smilingly and, turning to Millicent, said, "You have met my Honey, haven't you?"

Millicent smiled very, very sweetly and said she had. But, in spite of the smile, she somehow managed to convey to Honey at least that the experience had been a pretty dim and unimportant one.

They went into the big, bright cocktail lounge then, and John fetched drinks for them both. Millicent toyed charmingly with hers and was very amusing. It was quite astonishing how much she had managed to see during her few days in London, and she talked with witty penetration about a play which she and Dr. Anston had evidently both seen, while Honey strove to recall at least what the reviewers had said about it.

Before, however, she could contribute anything brilliant to the conversation, the subject changed once more, and she had to hear about a certain exhibition. From Millicent at least she gathered that if one had not visited it, one might just as well creep out and dig a hole and bury oneself.

At this point, fortunately, Dr. Anston himself assumed control of the conversation and, turning to Honey as though she were at least not subhuman, he asked her about her journey. This at least gave her a chance to speak, and Millicent perforce listened. But there was no gaucherie about the Eldon listening.

On the contrary, Millicent smiled faintly and indulgently, as though to say she could wait her turn. Meanwhile, of course, one could not expect anyone so naïve as Honey to have any conversation above the level of a railway timetable.

There is nothing more conducive to a display of dullness than someone else's bright conviction that one is dull. Honey, who was a charming and by no means unamusing person in her own circle, felt immediately that she was saying nothing worth the expenditure of the breath required to say it. And when her mother and Deborah finally appeared in the doorway of the cocktail lounge, she was hard put to it not to rush to them and welcome them with almost hysterical relief.

At this point Millicent smiled and drifted away. But even Honey's pleasure in her departure was tempered by the fact that Dr. Anston looked after Millicent with a slightly reflective air that seemed, at any rate to Honey's excited fancy, to contain an element of regret.

Plans for the evening were then discussed and, she thought perhaps by John's arrangement, it was decided that, although they would all four dine together, Honey and he would then go to a theater on their own.

"Of course you will want to have your first evening in London alone together," agreed Deborah, taking up her cue with almost too much understanding, and she looked at Honey so indulgently that Honey was almost hypnotized into giving John the shy, fond glance of a devoted financée.

Quite unnecessarily, he took that at its face value. And, as they all moved toward the palatial dining room, he drew Honey back slightly and said, "I'm glad you approve of the arrangement."

"I haven't said so," replied Honey, softly but rather severely because the thought of Millicent still rankled.

"But you looked volumes," he assured her, and laughed with altogether too much satisfaction, she thought.

All the same, Honey had to admit to herself that he looked remarkably attractive when he laughed like that. And, of course, she *was* glad that they were going out alone together afterward. If only because the arrangement would save her from the necessity of acting an exacting role before her mother and Deborah.

As it was, even the agreeable dinner party was a sufficient tax on her powers of acting and self-control. Her mother and Deborah vied with each other in plans. When Mrs. Milward once more brought up the question of an October wedding, Deborah accepted it with such enthusiasm that one might almost have supposed it were her own wedding she was planning.

"What does Honey say about that?" inquired John Anston, which Honey thought a poor form of support.

"I want to finish my training first," Honey said, almost curtly.

Deborah opened her lips, with every intention, Honey felt sure, of repeating all the protests that Mrs. Milward had already made on the train journey. But before she could utter any of them, her brother said, "Yes, I think you're right. I can't imagine your leaving any job unfinished, Honey. It would give you an unhappy and frustrated feeling, I'm sure."

Honey shot him a grateful glance at that, and in spite of some argument on the part of the other ladies, she was able to maintain her position with an air of reasonable good humor.

"Spring, then," Deborah said. "Spring is a lovely time for a wedding." And since Honey saw no reason (other than a marked lack of faith in English springs) to oppose this pleasant generalization, there was a great deal of enjoyable discussion leading nowhere, that served to bring them amicably as far as the coffee.

Over coffee, Deborah slightly shook Honey's composure with the announcement that she had arranged a large private party at the Gloria for the following evening. She said a few relations and many intimate friends would be looking forward to meeting John's fiancée there. She sounded excited.

But, calling on all her courage and resolution, Honey reminded herself that this, after all, was supposed to be one of the reasons for her trip to London. And so she managed to smile and say, "How *very* nice," in a charming and convincing manner.

After that, she and John made their escape. It was still early for the play they had chosen, and so he drove around the park to give Honey what he called a breath of country air in London. He also chose the occasion to ask quite solicitously, "Was there anything you wanted to ask me about?"

He was referring, she knew, to the party and the people his sister had arranged for her to meet. Or, if not that, then to any aspect of their position that she still wanted to discuss. But, in spite of that knowledge, in spite of the many questions she might have asked, in spite, even, of natural caution and tact that might well have restrained her, Honey could think of only one thing she wanted to query. Unbidden and irrepressible, the question rose to her lips.

"What do you think of Millicent Eldon?"

For a moment he looked surprised. Then, Honey was certain of it, a sort of amused reserve drew the faintest veil over the brightness of his glance.

"Millicent Eldon?" He appeared to give the subject his careless consideration. "I don't know that I've thought very much about her one way or the other, Honey. Why?"

Honey choked on the desire to tell him that, for a man who had given Millicent little thought, he had paid a great deal of attention to her. But she could not say that, of course. She could only mutter, a trifle sulkily, "I just wondered." And hoped he would leave it there.

But he carried the war into the enemy's camp with an air of merely continuing a subject that Honey had seen fit to introduce.

"What do you think of her?" he inquired politely.

What Honey thought of Millicent Eldon, of course, could not, with either policy or good manners, be put into words at that moment. And so, also adopting an air of considerable indifference toward the subject, she said carelessly, "Oh I don't know. I haven't seen much of her. But I did wonder why Deborah imagined she would make a suitable wife for you."

"Did you?" exclaimed John, and his tone of quite unwarrantable surprise reduced Honey to a condition of almost feverish curiosity and even anxiety.

"Why, d-do you think Deborah made a good choice, then?" She stammered slightly and wished desperately but unavailingly that she could leave this thorny subject alone.

"I think I made a better one." And gave her a quick, amused glance.

Honey was half-mollified, but only half.

"Deborah's intentions were serious," she pointed out.

"True. And, once I've disentangled you from this present situation, and Deborah returns to find me no longer engaged, she will probably open negotiations again," he said ruefully.

"Open...." Honey looked indescribably taken aback. "Do you mean try once more to push

Millicent onto you?" She looked at him, quite aghast.

"Why not?" asked John, with what Honey thought disgraceful equanimity.

"But would you like that?"

"I've learned to look at things as they are, Honey, not as I would wish them to be," he replied good humoredly.

"Don't be ridiculous!" cried Honey, greatly agitated. "Half the staff of St. Margaret's go in awe of you, and you pretend that you can't even protect yourself from marrying a girl you don't want."

"I never said that."

"But you ... you talked as though you might ... marry Millicent if your sister were sufficiently persistent."

"Oh no. I merely accepted the idea of Deborah's persistence philosophically," her companion corrected.

"If I married Millicent, it would not be because of anyone's insistence but my own."

Honey winced at the thought. She was not quite sure why.

"Then you mean you might marry Millicent because you wanted to?"

"For no other reason, I assure you. What have you against Millicent, Honey? You seem moved by the prospect."

Moved by it! Honey was appalled at the very idea. And yet, as he said, what had she really against the other girl, except that temperamentally they did not care for each other? Even that was of negligible importance. For, after the breaking of the engagement, presumably Honey would see little or nothing more of Dr. Anston or his associates.

But Millicent as Dr. Anston's wife! It was unthinkable. Honey's insides churned at the thought.

"I don't feel," Honey managed to say coldly, "that she is the right wife for you, that's all."

"Don't you, Honey?" He seemed inordinately interested. "Then you must feel you know me very well indeed."

Honey was silent.

"Well enough to choose the right wife for me. What type would you say? Tell me. I'm interested."

"You're nothing of the sort!" burst out Honey indignantly. "You're just teasing me."

"But, dear girl, why should I tease you? You and I are not on those terms at all," he insisted gravely. "Our attitude to each other is completely frank and realistic."

"Is it?" thought Honey, bewildered.

"I was quite serious in asking your opinion." He looked serious enough, and yet she had the idea that he trembled on the verge of a smile. "After the . . . amusing escapade we've shared, we probably do know a good deal about each other, don't you think?"

Did they? At this moment Honey felt that the Anston enigma had never been less clear to her.

"I don't know," she said soberly at last. "I don't believe anyone ever knows very much about you. The essential you, I mean. If you think you know a good deal about me, I daresay you're right. I'm not very complicated." She sighed a little, as she remembered how poorly Millicent had obviously rated her. "And I'm not very well suited for what you call an amusing escapade."

There was a faint quiver in her voice, because the phrase had hurt unaccountably. Perhaps he noticed that, for his tone changed subtly as he said, "Don't worry about it. You won't have to keep up the pretence much longer. It will all soon be over."

He must, she supposed, have meant that for consolation. And, indeed, the words in themselves should have been reassuring. But, somehow, his insistence that this would all soon be over had an anything but consoling effect upon Honey. She was hard put not to blink away a few tears when he dismissed the whole subject thus and observed that it was now time they drove to the theater.

The play was deservedly the most popular in London, and everyone around Honey seemed to enjoy themselves immensely. So did Dr. Anston. Only Honey herself seemed to find the full pleasure and point escape her, and a great deal of the time she sat there wondering about the future—Dr. Anston's future as well as her own, which was really rather officious of her, considering that he was really no affair of hers.

Afterward they went out to supper. Honey cheered up somewhat, and they had a good time. He told her that the party the following evening would be the only occasion when she would be expected to be on show. Otherwise she was to enjoy herself like any other "happily unengaged girl."

In this, however, he had counted without Mrs. Milward and his sister. For the next day Honey spent a somewhat agitating time finding reasons why they should not buy a variety of things for her trousseau.

"It's never wise to leave everything until the last minute, darling," insisted Mrs. Milward, who adored a shopping spree and seldom had the chance of enjoying one.

But Honey asserted with some reason that there was plenty of time left between now and the proposed spring wedding.

"I shall bring some things back from the States with me," declared Deborah happily, refusing to listen to any of Honey's polite protests about this.

"Well, I can't help it. I've done my best," thought Honey impatiently. "She'll just have to give them to someone else."

For a moment a dreadful thought entered her mind, then she dismissed it with a sigh of relief, reflecting with unworthy but understandable pleasure that everything would be just a couple of sizes too small for Millicent.

In the afternoon she was allowed to rest, in preparation for the party. And since, like most nurses, Honey could sleep any time and anywhere, she did rest completely. She woke up entirely refreshed, with her courage, her spirits, and even her sense of humor keyed to accept the challenge that the evening might present.

No longer did she feel nervous, or only very slightly nervous, about meeting the relatives and friends. No longer did she even mind the fact that Millicent would inevitably be at the party. She thought...."He said himself that he thought he made a better choice than Deborah did. And it wasn't entirely a joke. Or, if it was, I'll show him."

She got off the bed, pulled back the curtains and went to look at herself in the mirror. Even with her fair hair tumbled and her face innocent of makeup, there was a sweet, youthful tenderness about the young girl who looked back at Honey from the mirror.

"Not bad," thought Honey, a slight fugitive dimple appearing for a moment in one cheek. "Not bad. At least I'll show him there's better fish in the sea than Millicent. And if that's the only thing I ever do for him, I shall have done him a very good turn."

Fired with this missionary spirit for rescuing Dr. Anston from himself, Honey made her preparations. And when at last she stood ready, in the green and gold short taffeta dress that she and her mother had bought that morning, she felt and looked not ill-equipped for the fray.

She wished she had something just a trifle more imposing than her single-strand pearl necklace to wear, but it would have to do. At least she had her ring, her truly wonderful ring. Honey looked at it affectionately and then, on irresistible impulse, pressed the hand that wore it against her cheek, in a little gesture of tenderness that was partly for the most beautiful thing that had ever been given her, and just a little bit for the giver.

Then her mother entered the room, stopped, cast a look of maternal pride upon her child and murmuring, "Lovely, lovely!!!" twitched one or two folds of the dress into what she considered better line.

"Now, here is the finishing touch to your outfit," she declared and, opening a small box she was carrying, she disclosed to Honey's enchanted gaze a beautifully wrought antique necklace of dark yellow topaz set in gold, glowing in its velvet setting.

"Mother *darling!*" Honey embraced her mother. "How wonderful! It's exactly, exactly what I want."

"Well, you must thank John just as nicely," Mrs. Milward said with a smile. "For it's really his present, though he took me with him to choose it this afternoon, so that he would be sure to get something to suit your dress tonight."

"John bought it for me?"

"Yes. He said he wanted you to have something to remember this evening by."

"He said that?"

"Yes. Though I don't imagine," Mrs. Milward went on with an air of slightly sentimental satisfaction, "that it will be an evening we're any of us likely to forget, in any case."

"No," said Honey, stirred by a sense of curious, almost prophetic conviction. "I'm sure I'll remember it all my life."

Then she silently unfastened her string of pearls and replaced them by the beautiful flat topaz necklace that seemed to cast a faint golden glow on the creamy skin of her neck and throat.

"I'm ready," she said quietly to her mother, and they went downstairs together. Deborah, who was a natural party-giver, had engaged one of the Gloria's private rooms for the occasion. At one end the table was set for about 20 people, but there was also ample space to sit and talk beforehand, while drinks were served and introductions made.

A few guests had already arrived, and Honey was aware, as she made her entrance, that a subtle impression of approval emanated from the small company. She could not have said just how she knew it, but it was as heady as wine and made her more determined than ever to play her part well.

Deborah and John came forward to greet her and her mother and, whether for the benefit of her audience or her own inexplicable pleasure she was not sure, Honey raised her face to John and said, "Thank you, darling, for the wonderful necklace. I'll remember this evening—and you—every time I put it on."

He kissed her upturned face and whispered, "I'll hold you to that."

And then Deborah wafted her on to meet Uncle This and Aunt That and my old friend So-and-So.

To Honey's mingled amusement, embarrassment and pleasure, Sir Brian Allwood, the senior visiting surgeon at St. Margaret's, was among those to whom she was presented. A very handsome man in his early sixties, Sir Brian was known for his informal manner. And more than one distracted nurse had been rescued from the depths of despair and gone on to pursue a useful career, because he had smiled or commented genially from his Olympian heights on some first-year inadequacy that had previously seemed sufficient reason for suicide.

"So you're the girl Anston is going to marry." He took Honey's hand and surveyed her with his shrewd, handsome eyes. "Very good taste he shows, too. In my view surgeons should always marry nurses. I did it myself and never regretted it."

Honey laughed and colored.

"Thank you, sir," she said demurely. "I naturally like to support that view. But why do you think they should?"

"Keeps them in the profession in their private life as well as their public life. Otherwise they get caught by social climbers and that's fatal. Good-looking surgeons are the first choice of social climbers, you know. Best stepping-stones to a distinguished position."

"I suppose you're right," agreed Honey thoughtfully, and her glance went to Millicent, who had just entered.

"I'm sure of it," declared Sir Brian with a twinkle. "I speak from experience. But Anston will do very well with you, my dear. Very well. Even Sister speaks well of you occasionally."

"Does she?" exclaimed Honey, flattered beyond belief.

"But don't tell her I gave her away," said the famous surgeon, with the very slightest suspicion of a wink. And, laughing a good deal, Honey went on to be presented to other guests, stimulated and gratified by Sir Brian's obvious approval.

Whether or not this auspicious beginning was responsible Honey could not have said, but from the moment Sir Brian shook hands with her, she knew she was a success.

She knew it from the approving smiles and glances that followed her everywhere. She knew it from her mother's deprecating air of not wishing to claim anything outstanding for her child but.... She knew it from Millicent's slightly narrowed glance and brittle smile. And she knew it from the way John's keen, light eyes rested upon her with a mixture of amused appreciation and interest.

At dinner Honey sat between John and Sir Brian.

And if the nurse part of her almost fainted at the thought of such exalted buttressing, the Honey part of her enjoyed it immensely. She sparkled and made amusing little jokes; yet she displayed such gentleness and warmth. Everyone there, with the probable exception of Millicent, could not help feeling that, if they were ever seriously ill, they would like to be nursed by this fair-haired, dark-eyed girl that John Anston had very sensibly captured.

It could not have gone better, Honey knew. Except that perhaps it went too well. Too well for any party that ushered in an engagement already scheduled for early breaking.

But she thrust the thought of that aside. It would only shake her nerve if she allowed herself to think of reality. For one evening at least she would enjoy her fancied romance. And if it lifted her spirits a little too high and made her heart beat a trifle too fast, well, all the tomorrows were waiting, with their sober routine and their ruthless common sense, so that one evening snatched from their stern realities could not be grudged to her.

After dinner the older guests sat and talked or played bridge, but the younger ones took themselves off to the Gloria's glittering ballroom, where Honey discovered that Dr. Anston was an excellent dancer.

He seemed equally pleased with her performance. And presently, as he piloted her around the great circular room, he said, "You were wonderful, Honey. I never saw anyone play the part of a happily engaged girl better. I was inundated with congratulations, and I tremble to think what they will all think of my good sense when I let you slip through my fingers later."

"Don't let's think about that now," she begged him quickly. "Tonight is . . . is something special, even if it isn't quite real. Let's enjoy it and leave the problems for tomorrow."

"An excellent idea," he agreed and lightly touched his lips to the smooth curve of her cheek.

And after that he too seemed to yield to some romantic, reckless mood of gaiety, teasing her and making laughing love to her, until she could hardly believe that this was the respected and feared Dr. Anston of St. Margaret's. Still less, could she decide if he were flirting with her in his own right, or merely carrying out his pretended role with artistic thoroughness.

She began to be just a little bit afraid. Not of him but of herself. It would be silly to let her head be turned by all the success and admiration she had received. And it was even sillier not to be able to control the rising pulse of excitement within her. She reminded herself that she had had his arm around her before, and yet she had not felt this strange quivering enjoyment at the contact.

He was handsome, of course, and distinguished, and the kind of man women turned to look at. But she must remember he was not really hers in any sense; that she had no right to feel this heady, proprietorial dazzlement when he looked down at her and smiled in that bright-eyed, provocative way.

"I think I'd rather not dance the next one," she said, as the music stopped. He yielded immediately, but whereas she had meant to seek out her mother and Deborah, he led her to one of the small sitting-out rooms. The sound of the band reached them only faintly and the outside world seemed suddenly shut off.

"Are you tired?" he asked solicitously and led her over to a window seat out of the sight of the crowd.

"Not really, no." Compelled by some inner excitement, she remained standing. "I just thought . . . I just wanted. . . .We seemed t-to be overplaying our roles." She stammered in a sort of eager confusion. "I thought if we were alone and not under observation, I mean—we could just be natural and sensible."

"You thought that being alone would have the effect of making us behave sensibly? Oh, Honey! That's treason against all the laws of romance," he declared, taking both her hands and laughing down at her reproachfully. "I assure you that being alone with you doesn't have that effect on me at all."

"No . . . please. . . ." She tried to pull her hands away, but the beautiful hands whose strength she had often admired held hers easily, though lightly. "I don't want to go on with this!" Inexplicable panic gripped her, as though she suddenly saw unsuspected breakers ahead. "I want to stop the whole thing—now."

"But you can't, my dear." His voice was quiet but oddly compelling. "Tonight is something special, even if it isn't quite real. Those are your own words, and I won't have you take them back now."

She started to say something else in protest. But, suddenly releasing her hands, he caught her in his arms, bent her back slightly and kissed her full on her mouth.

It was not a light or laughing kiss. It carried their

make-believe to the very edge of reality. And in that moment Honey felt the bright bubble of illusion burst into a thousand rainbow fragments, leaving her with one cold, startling, almost terrifying fact. She *wanted* him to kiss her like that, and she did not want it to be part of the "amusing escapade."

"Let me go," she said in a whisper. And because he did not immediately release her, all her fear of her new and shattering discovery swept over her afresh.

Nothing mattered except that he should release her and that she should somehow escape from a situation entirely beyond her own managing. She was done with laughing and make-believe. She must get away from him if not from herself. Already a great gulf yawned between the Honey she had been and the frightened, sobered girl she now was.

"Let me go," she said again almost fiercely. And quite forgetting that she was a third-year nurse and he a famous surgeon whom she called "sir" in her saner moments, she raised her hand and gave his distinguished cheek a sharp slap.

The effect was instantaneous. He let her go and stepped back with an exclamation that was not entirely gentlemanly. His gray eyes looked light and angry. They shone with a defiant brilliance she had never seen before.

For perhaps two seconds they faced each other in silence. And then, as both drew breath to voice their anger, Deborah came hurrying into the room, so full of her own affairs that she did not even notice the tense attitude or the curious silence of the two she sought.

"John! Such excitement," she cried, with

unconscious truth. "I've just had a call from New York. Ronald wants me back there next week. But next week, my dear! I'm to fly over on Sunday night. He can't manage all the settling up without me. I knew he couldn't, bless him! But I'll be back. We'll be back all the sooner. Isn't it wonderful?"

"Wonderful," her brother agreed mechanically, but as though he were thinking of something else—which no doubt he was.

"I'm so glad, dear, that at least I was here for your engagement party." Deborah turned to the pale, silent Honey. "I should have hated to miss that. Don't do anything too thrilling before I come back, will you?" She laughed. "And then we'll start the real preparations for the wedding."

Perhaps it was the vista of further complications that these words conjured up. Perhaps it was simply that she was still frightened and angry by the previous scene. Or perhaps she suddenly saw a quick, ruthless, effective way of extricating herself from an unbearable situation.

Whatever it was, a cool, calm decision came to Honey in that moment, and, raising her dark eyes, she looked almost kindly at Deborah and said, "I'm sorry, Deborah. We won't do anything of the sort. The engagement is over."

CHAPTER EIGHT

"I DON'T understand." Deborah looked helplessly from her brother to Honey and back again. "The engagement, over? But it can't be! It's only just begun. Aren't you well, Honey dear? Has something . . . something happened?" She stammered slightly in her incredulous dismay.

For a moment Honey was overwhelmed by a sort of desperate remorse. It was wrong to shatter anyone's serenity with such dreadful finality, and she almost yielded to the temptation to take back what she had said—to reassure poor Deborah with almost any argument or pretence that would hide the tatters of this torn romance.

But she had had enough of pretence. She had been too shocked and frightened by that moment of revelation when pretence had seemed more precious than any reality. She had known that her whole scale of values had slipped out of gear.

"I'm sorry, Deborah," she said again, as though there were some necessity for her to apologize to someone for her broken engagement. "I know it must be a shock. But Dr. Anston and I—John and I—are not going on with the engagement."

"Dr. Anston," repeated Deborah dazedly, as though in Honey's extraordinary way of referring to her fiancé she might find the key to this mystery. As, indeed, she might. "But you were so happy, such a success. Everyone was enchanted with you, Honey, and so happy for John and . . . and me. I can't—I simply can't—go out there now and tell them all it's a mistake."

"There's no necessity to do that, Deborah." Her brother spoke at last, but in an odd, chilled way that sounded expressionless. "There's no need to tell anyone tonight. That would be unnecessarily sensational. We can arrange things quietly in a few days' time."

"Then you mean it's *true?*"

"I'm afraid so."

Deborah, who had apparently clung to some remnant of the idea that it might be a mistake, seemed to sag, almost physically, at this confirmation by her brother.

"I can't understand it." She fiddled aimlessly with the clasp of her evening bag and looked almost as though she might begin to cry. "I can't understand it at all."

"Don't try to," her brother told her curtly but not unkindly.

"But I'm much older than both of you. You mustn't think I'm interfering if I say that there's no quarrel that can't be made up if two people love each other," Deborah said earnestly.

"I believe you." Her brother wearily passed his hand over his face and looked suddenly as though he had had very much more than enough of this scene. "But the operative clause there is—if they love each other. Honey and I don't love each other. . . ."

"We only pretended to do so. I'm sorry. The idea was mine. And a damned bad idea it was, too."

"Do you mind," said Honey in a strangled voice, "if I go now? I don't think I can bear to stay and hear it all discussed again. Make some excuse for me, please —any excuse—if people miss me. Say I'm ill—faint— anything. But don't ask me to go back among them all and pretend any more."

And, without even waiting for Deborah or John Anston either to agree or protest, she turned and almost ran from the room.

By good luck rather than calculation, she found herself near a staircase. Not the big main stairway, where she had lingered watching Dr. Anston and Millicent—could it be only yesterday—but a narrower staircase at the back of the hotel.

Possessed by an illogical fear that, even now, someone might pursue her and insist on her returning to the scene of her triumph and her despair, Honey raced up to the second floor. And after some frantic wandering around what seemed like miles of corridor, she stumbled at last on her own room.

She had not her key with her, but a friendly chambermaid opened the door for her, making some good-humored comment to which Honey somehow managed to reply coherently. And then the door was closed again, shutting out the maid and all the world. Honey was alone at last. Except for her thoughts.

She leaned against the door for a minute or two, with her eyes closed, aware only of the relief of not having to face people or to pretend any more.

But slowly the weight of her own wretchedness made it seem an effort even to stand. Rather stiffly she moved away from the door and mechanically began to strip off her beautiful dress, her necklace, she sobbed a little at that point though she hardly knew it, and then her other clothes.

Then wrapping herself in her dressing gown, she flung herself across the bed, face downward, as though she would blot out even the sight of the impersonal hotel bedroom.

It was over. The hateful, beloved, fascinating, frightening engagement with Dr. Annston was over. Ruthlessly she had cut all the bonds. And, if the ends hung uneven and unconnected, at least there was nothing to hold her any longer. Nothing except—she raised her head and stared at her hand—nothing except her ring.

The moment had come to take that off now. Return it to him with a polite little note. It had never represented anything real. Now it did not even represent their make-believe. For that too was over.

She fingered the ring nervously, as though to draw it from her hand. But, instead of doing that, she suddenly bowed her bright head on her clenched fingers and wept unrestrainedly.

For what she could not quite have said. Only that it was all over.

Some time later her mother came and knocked on the door. It was Honey's impulse to say, "Go away." But she had precipitated this crisis and must deal with it. So, wiping the tears from her cheeks, she sat up and called, "Come in."

Her mother entered. Her pretty, eager, bewildered face a study. Honey's heart smote her. For it was not only her own plans and hopes that lay in ruins.

"Honey. . . ." Her mother came over and sat on the bed beside her, without attempting to touch her, "What's happened, darling?"

She was glad her mother did not embrace her emotionally or otherwise increase the tension of the scene. In some curious way, it was comforting to be spoken to so quietly and yet lovingly, as though one were a lost child. Which perhaps she was.

"The engagement is over," Honey said, and she was surprised at the quiet finality of her own voice.

Her mother bit her lip, but did not break out into the protests that Honey had steeled herself to face. All she said was "Aren't you going to tell me why?"

"If you like." Honey pushed back her heavy, fair hair wearily. "It was all a mistake, anyway. The engagement, I mean. It was never real."

Mrs. Milward swallowed. In her experience people did not become engaged by mistake, and she found this very difficult to accept.

"Couldn't you tell me a little more than that, dear?" she pleaded. "It all seemed quite emphatically real to me, and I think to everyone else too."

Honey smiled very faintly.

"That was because we acted so well," she said with a sigh. And then she thought suddenly how wonderful it would be to tell someone the whole story. Someone who wouldn't criticize or blame one, or point out the self-evident fact that she had been crazy ever to embark on such a project. Someone whose dear partiality would gloss over all one's foolishness and mistakes.

"Oh, *Mother!*" Honey cried, in the tone of one who has broken her doll and cut her knee only to realize that she is not a big girl after all. And, flinging her arms around her mother, she leaned her head against her and began to pour out the whole story. Right from the beginning, at the group meeting of the Women's Institute, when everyone had just assumed that she and Dr. Anston were more or less engaged.

"I know I was silly ever to take it on," she admitted humbly, "and sometimes I wanted to turn back. But there never seemed to be a chance, Mother."

"It was all Miss Emms's fault," declared Mrs. Milward indignantly and, one feels bound to say, unjustly.

"Oh, Mother!" Even in her distress, Honey was intrigued though not convinced by this novel point of view. "How could it be, poor thing?"

"It was she who started the gossip," Mrs. Milward said firmly. "Why, she stopped your father and told him you were engaged, even before you knew it yourself. Don't you remember?"

"We-ell, she scooped the news, if you like," Honey conceded, with a pale smile. "But I don't think we can blame anyone but our two selves for what really happened."

"I must say I am astonished at John." Mrs. Milward spoke reluctantly, for she hated blaming anyone of whom she was so unfeignedly fond. But, as the only alternative culprit to Honey herself, he had to be sacrificed.

"Oh, I don't know." Honey sprang to the erring Dr. Anston's defence with unnecessary eagerness. "We were both responsible for this stupid scheme. . . ."

"But it was to please him originally. And it was carried much too far. That handsome ring!" Mrs. Milward glanced at Honey's hand. "That lovely necklace this afternoon." She looked around the room.

"I've taken off the necklace," Honey said abruptly.

"And the ring, dear? You should take that off too, you know, now your engagement is broken."

"I know," Honey said, but she curled her fingers tightly into the palm of her hand, as though she thought something or someone might remove the ring by force.

"I mean to . . . soon."

"And then what?" Mrs. Milward sighed, and Honey was completely dumb, for suddenly those three words opened a vista of such a pointless, loveless, empty future that a great lump rose in her throat and nearly choked her.

For a minute or two both of them were silent. Then Mrs. Milward said, as though reluctantly making the best of a very heavy burden. "Well, it's something, I suppose, that there are no deep feelings involved on either side. All we have to deal with is social embarrassment and disappointment."

"Yes," murmured Honey huskily.

"Deborah's immediate departure to the States is almost providential, in the circumstances. It saves her from having to make any explanations to her friends and relations for a little while. And it also gives us a very good reason for returning home tomorrow."

"Tomorrow!" For some inexplicable reason, Honey looked aghast at this.

"Well, of course, my dear. We can hardly stay on here as the guests of John's sister if you're not going to marry him, after all."

"No, I suppose not."

"In any case—" Mrs. Milward looked puzzledly at her daughter "—I would have thought it would mean less embarrassment for you if we returned home."

"Yes, of course," Honey said and immediately began to wonder feverishly what likelihood there was of her seeing John again before their departure.

"Well, you'd better get to bed now, darling." Her mother drew a slight, involuntary sigh. "It's late."

"Yes," Honey agreed, though she shrank from being left alone to struggle with her own unhappy thoughts once more. "Thank you, Mother, for being so understanding."

"My dear child! Who would understand if your own mother doesn't?" exclaimed Mrs. Milward, with some feeling. "Though I'm bound to say," she added generously, "that Deborah behaved very well about it all."

"Did she have to explain to many people?" asked Honey, who could not quite control a reluctant yet fascinated curiosity about the situation that she had left behind her when she had fled upstairs.

"She didn't explain the *real* facts to anyone. She merely made graceful excuses to the few people who inquired about your absence."

"Was it very difficult?"

"Not as difficult as one might have supposed." Mrs. Milward determinedly made light of Deborah's and her own difficulties. "Several of the older guests had already gone, and most of the others were dancing in the ballroom. That's the advantage of having a party at anywhere like the Gloria. Once people start dancing, they become absorbed in their own affairs and don't look around too searchingly for other members of the party."

"I suppose you're right," agreed Honey, with a slight, irrepressible pang of envy for such single-minded and carefree pleasure.

Then her mother went away into her own room. And there was nothing for Honey to do but get into bed and lie there; thinking of the extraordinary past and the strangely empty future.

With a loving efficiency that seemed almost to wall

Honey around, her mother attended next day to every detail of their departure. Miraculously she dealt with inquiries, casual or particular. Tactfully she settled whatever it was necessary to settle with Deborah. And speedily she repacked and arranged for them to depart by a train soon after breakfast.

"Don't you think I ought to see Deborah?" Honey suggested, over breakfast in her room.

But her mother shook her head.

"It isn't necessary, child. Deborah understands just exactly how you feel about it all. . . ."

"How can she?" thought Honey. "I don't understand it myself."

"And she knows that, although you don't blame John," went on Mrs. Milward magnanimously, "any meeting would be pointless and painful just now."

Honey wanted passionately to say that her mother had gone rather far if she had been as emphatic as that. But what good was it to dispute the details of the break? In any case, perhaps her mother was right. It was difficult to see how any meeting could do anyone a service.

Only, as Honey and her mother passed through the great foyer of the Gloria on their way out, Honey glanced around with almost desperate eagerness. And it was not Deborah she was seeking.

Symbolically perhaps, the only person in sight whom she knew was Millicent. And even she was talking animatedly to someone else and did not notice Honey's departure. It was as though a door closed behind her, shutting off everything to do with Dr. Anston and his private circle.

In the train, Honey inevitably found her thoughts

running anxiously ahead, to meet the next crisis. And, looking across nervously at her mother, she said, "I don't know how we're going to explain our sudden return to Daddy."

"I have explained," her mother replied composedly. "I telephoned to him last night."

"Oh, Mother, did you? Did you tell him about the broken engagement?"

"No. I merely told him that Deborah had to return to the States immediately, and that we were therefore, of course, cutting our visit short."

"How did he sound on the phone when you told him that?"

"Like a man on a desert island who sees a sail on the horizon," replied Mrs. Milward indulgently. "Your father is a man who likes to have his women-folk around him."

Honey laughed a little and then sighed enviously in the mistaken, but quite common, belief that one's parents don't really know what heartbreak is.

"Then you didn't mention about me at all?"

"No. For one thing, the thing went 'pip-pip,' which always demoralizes me. And, for another, I didn't really know at what point you intended to make the break public."

sity of making a definite decision pressed upon her, she looked at her mother in some distress.

"I don't think there's any special hurry," Mrs. Milward said, with a steadying calm. "I see no reason why you shouldn't finish your few days' leave quietly at home now, without any crisis atmosphere. Then, when you've gone back to the hospital, I'll tell your father all about it. At least, I will tell him as much as he will understand," she added, in kindly but firm qualification. She smiled softly at her daughter.

"Oh, Mother!" Honey felt overwhelmed with gratitude. Can you really put it off until then?"

"Of course, darling." Her mother smiled. "When you've been married as long as I have, you get to know that tactful timing smoothes out most family crises."

"I expect you're right," Honey agreed soberly.

And then she fell to wondering if her own timing, in relation to the breaking of her engagement, had shown any of the tact that her mother so justly regarded as important.

If she had not panicked so stupidly because Dr. Anston kissed her—or, more exactly, because of the way she felt when Dr. Anston kissed her—she might still be in London enjoying her fictitious engagement. Though whether or not that would have been an advantage, she was not able to decide at this moment.

They arrived home in the early afternoon by taxi, since Mr. Milward could not get away to meet them at the station. Honey's first impression was that the delicious, uneventful peace of one's own home was the most heavenly thing in the world.

But, once she had unpacked her things, had an early supper with her mother, and looked around the garden, the dreadful conviction began to grow upon her that delicious and uneventful peace was not at all what she wanted.

During the last few weeks she had lived in a state of perpetual excitement and anxiety. If she had had to give an opinion at the time, she would have declared, of course, that it was a most harrowing way of life and that it was altogether too bad that she had had that situation thrust upon her.

But now, now that she had nothing to worry about, no anxiety lest some fresh crisis should involve Dr. Anston and herself, she wondered bewilderedly how she had lived so busily and happily before he had entered her life.

That was what it always came back to: Dr. Anston and the way her life had centered around him recently. If only she had been a little less precipitate. If only. . . . But she refused to let her fancy follow that dangerous path. Better accept the situation as it was and decide, first of all, how she was going to meet her father's affectionate inquiries, and then, much worse, the comments and questions of her friends and colleagues when she returned to the hospital.

In spite of some reflective, and even disquieted, glances from her mother, Honey was still wearing her engagement ring. How else, she asked herself, was she to substantiate to her father the theory that she was still engaged?

But even this precious delay could last no more than a few days. When her leave was up and she returned to the hospital, she would have to take off her ring and face the consequent astonishment and curiosity.

The meeting with her father was not difficult. He was inclined to think that whatever her mother did was right, and so he expressed sympathy for the abrupt curtailing of their pleasure, while quite obviously delighting in their unexpectedly early return. And then, apart from commenting somewhat unwisely on the fact that they did not seem to have managed to spend much money, he had little more to say.

But even he might have detected some inexplicable

depression in his daughter's manner, and suspected complications, if a rival claim on all their interests had not presented itself.

Heralded by no more than a telegram, delivered in person by an excited Miss Morris from the post office earlier in the evening, Michael arrived home very late that night.

"But, darling—" Mrs. Milward flung her arms around him and blinked away a tear—"I thought you were building a bridge in darkest Africa or something."

"A generator," he corrected her kindly, "and not in darkest Africa. Quite near civilization."

"It's the same thing," Mrs. Milward said happily. And, being a kind fellow, her son did not insist on pointing out that it was entirely different. He merely explained modestly that, owing to some pretty good work on the part of himself and his team, they had finished well ahead of schedule.

Even Honey's heart felt lighter at the sight of her tall, carefree, affectionate brother. And he had so much to tell them all that, for a while at least, she managed to put off his questions about her engagement almost casually, with the promise that they would talk of that later.

"The subject requires a whole session on its own, I guess." Her brother smiled at her good-humoredly. "But at any rate tell me who it is, Honey."

"John Anston."

"One of the surgeons at the hospital," her father amplified. "An exceptionally good fellow."

"But I thought that was the chap you wrote about in your last letter but one," Honey's brother said, with an exactness of recollection that might be flattering but on this occasion, was slightly embarrassing. "You said then that he was a perfect stinker, or words to that effect."

"I changed my mind," Honey explained, coloring slightly, while her father laughed a good deal and her mother looked unusually grave.

Michael gave his father a man-to-man grin at this and remarked maddeningly that he believed nurses always fell in love with their surgeons at some point or another.

"They don't, you know," said Honey almost coldly.

"Well, you're not in a very good position to argue that one," her brother told her amusedly. "Look what you've done."

At this Honey smiled with as good a grace as she could. She tried to look like the happily engaged girl who hardly minded what jokes were made at her expense. Her brother, satisfied that all was well with his dearly loved Honey, turned once more to his parents and began to explain in great detail just how it was he had managed to finish his generator ahead of time and thus surprise them in this delightful manner.

And, if they nodded their heads and looked very wise and knowledgeable, without really understanding much of what he was saying, they were doing no more than the rest of us do when a beloved person insists on embarking upon technical explanations that have no interest at all for us, apart from their connection with the speaker.

With relief, as well as sisterly partiality, Honey saw thankfully that the household was probably going to revolve around her brother during the next few days. If that were the case, perhaps she might dare to hope that her own miserably tangled affairs would escape any great degree of comment or question from them.

But, again, as soon as one had been virtually dealt with, one had to look ahead anxiously to the next one. And right in front of Honey loomed the worst crisis of all. The dreadful necessity of returning to the hospital no longer engaged to Dr. Anston.

She lay awake for a long time that night, trying to steel herself against the thought of the astonished and pitying glances she would have to encounter; not to mention the point-blank questioning there would be from some of her less delicate minded colleagues.

And then, toward morning, she arrived at a partial solution of the problem. She decided that she would telephone Barbara sometime during the day, tell her of the broken engagement, and ask her to pass on the news as tactfully as she could, with the firm indication that Honey wanted no questions on the subject.

It was not a very brave way of dealing with the situation, Honey knew. But she felt she had just about had enough of being brave, bright, and resourceful. And, in any case, she knew that Barbara would shoulder the task with friendly willingness.

Even this was something she shrank from doing. But, early that afternoon, when she knew Barbara would be off duty, her brother was safely out of the house, and even her sympathetic mother was somewhere in the garden, Honey summoned all her resolution, telephoned the residence and asked for Barbara.

As she stood there, holding the telephone in her hand and trying not to notice how heavily her heart was thumping, she felt a cowardly hope rise within her that Barbara might be out. But someone picked up the receiver at the other end, and Barbara's voice said, "Hello."

"H-hello," replied Honey a little unsteadily. "This is Milward. Honey—"

"*Honey!* Are you speaking from London?"

"No. I'm speaking from home."

"But I thought. . . ."

"Yes, I know. We came back sooner than we intended. Dr. An—John's sister had to go back to the States unexpectedly. And anyway, the engagement is off. That's what I called up to tell you." She rushed on so that Barbara could not unnerve her with exclamations and interruptions. "I'll tell you something about it when I come back. But will you let the others know, Barbara, and please tell them that I don't want any questions or commiseration. Not any."

There was a long silence at the other end.

"Are you still there?" asked Honey timidly.

"Yes, of course. I was just wondering what to say. If you don't want either questions or commiseration—"

"Oh, I didn't mean that for you personally, Barbara! Though, of course, one can't say anything much on the phone."

"N-no. But can I at least ask if, well, did you do the breaking off, or did he?"

"Oh, I did," Honey explained, more forlornly than she knew.

"I see. But are you absolutely sure about this, Honey? Wouldn't you rather I delayed telling—"

"Absolutely sure," insisted Honey. "I don't know that it is such a complete surprise for me."

"You mean you never thought it would work?"

"I don't mean that at all. To tell the truth, in an odd way, I thought it *would* work. Once I'd recovered from the initial surprise, I mean." Again, a long silence.

"But then, " with difficulty Honey kept her voice steady, "how could you guess that anything had gone wrong?"

"I suppose it was just the way Dr. Anston looked when I saw him this morning."

"You . . . you saw him this morning?" stammered Honey. "Where?"

"In the hospital, of course."

"But it isn't his day for operating."

"Not his regular day, no. But he was summoned for an emergency. There was a consultation this morning and he's operating this afternoon. One of those three or four-hour touches, I believe it is."

Honey was bereft of speech. For there rose before her such a clear picture of Dr. Anston in the operating room. She could almost see the glint of his cool gray eyes above the surgeon's mask, and the incredibly delicate movements of the long, strong hands in the surgeon's gloves.

And she wished she could be there with him. With a nostalgic longing, amounting almost to passion, she wanted to be with him wherever he was. In the operating room, in London, in Meadlands. It didn't matter where, because, wherever he was, there was the center of her world.

CHAPTER NINE

"ARE you still there?" It was Barbara who asked the question this time.

"Yes of course. What did you mean, Barbara, when you said you thought something might be wrong, from the way Dr. Anston looked? *How* did he look?"

"I don't know quite how to describe it. Grim and remote and . . . dispirited. I don't ever remember seeing him look that way before. Grim and remote, but not the other thing."

Honey bit her lip and didn't manage to say anything in reply to that. She could only think how very badly she had managed everything.

"Is it quite beyond mending, Honey?" Barbara inquired, after a few moments' silence.

"I'm afraid so."

"You've returned your ring and everything?"

Honey glanced guiltily at the bright circlet on her finger. But it would be too ridiculous to say, after all her protests and assertions, that she was still wearing Dr. Anston's ring. So, hastily, and quite untruthfully, she said, "Oh yes!" and immediately decided that she must somehow find some way of turning intention into fact as soon as possible.

In spirit, the gesture had unquestionably been made. In practical form it must now be completed.

"Well," Barbara was saying, "I'm terribly sorry about it all, and I can imagine you're feeling pretty depressed at the moment. But you know your own affairs best, I don't doubt, and there's nothing helpful one can say. Particularly if you'd rather not talk about it anyway. I'll tell the others for you, though, if that's really what you want."

Honey said unhappily that this was indeed what she wanted. Then she thanked Barbara for taking on an awkward task and replaced the receiver. Her mind was still very much on what she had just been told about Dr. Anston's mood that morning.

So he was at the hospital! Not more than 20 miles away. Although, of course, this meant nothing at all when they were a thousand miles apart in all that mattered. It was no use lingering nostalgically over that thought, she told herself. She must now give her whole attention to the practical problem of returning his ring to him, thus making the situation as final as she had already described it.

One could send it back by registered mail, of course, accompanied by a cool and dignified little note. But Honey blanched at the thought of Miss Morris's reaction if she were to present herself at the post office with a significantly small parcel addressed to Dr. Anston.

There must be another way, a better way.

The excited color flooded into Honey's face. She glanced at her watch and then stood there perfectly still in the sunlit hall for a moment, as though frightened by her own inspiration.

In ten minutes' time the local bus would be passing the end of the road. In less than an hour it would be in Forchester. *She* could be in Forchester, where Dr. Anston was.

He would still be operating, in all probability. But

even the longest operation does come to an end at last. He would be free then to accept his ring from her hands, and to exchange with her whatever words still remained to be said about this whole sorry business.

"It's better than just finishing everything with a formal note," Honey told herself almost feverishly. "He owes it to me to at least . . . no, perhaps I owe it to him. Well, anyway, it doesn't matter which way around it should be. It only matters that I should see him and speak to him once more. Not as Nurse Milward, but as Honey."

She whirled around and ran out into the garden at the back of the house.

"Mother, Mother! I've just remembered something I have to do in town," she called to her mother, industriously weeding near the bottom of the garden. "I can catch the three o'clock bus, if I hurry. I'll be back for dinner, I think. But I must run now!"

Before her mother could call back any more than the "Very well, dear" of all well-trained or naturally understanding mothers, Honey had turned once more, rushed through the house, grabbing her purse and gloves as she ran, banging the front door behind her.

As she ran down the road, she saw Miss Emms coming toward her, on the other side. But nothing was going to stop Honey now. Not even Miss Emms in search of information. She waved with false cheerfulness as she passed and ran on, aware that Miss Emms stood and looked after her, undoubtedly asking herself what Honey Milward could be doing, tearing along the road like that on a warm afternoon.

With two minutes to spare, she caught the Forchester bus, more than half-empty at this time in the afternoon. Only a matter of minutes after the great decision had been made, she was jogging along the road she had so often traveled to and from the hospital.

Sitting in the front seat, she now had time to review the position and consider her plan of action. As she did so, her first ardor began to cool.

In the hall at home seemingly all she had to do was to make sure that she caught the bus and go to Dr. Anston. Now, she saw, she might well travel the first 20 miles of her journey with ease. But then, how did one bridge the final gulf?

How was she a nurse out of uniform and supposedly on leave, in any case, to find her way to the side of a busy and distinguished surgeon, who did not even know that she was coming and probably would not want to see her if he did?

Honey glanced down self-consciously at her dress. Pretty, informal, highly suitable for an afternoon at home or in the garden, but almost as conspicuous as a bathing suit in hospital corridors on a non-visiting day.

"I'll simply have to slip into the residence and change into uniform," she thought, slightly surprised herself at the coolness of her planning. "And then. . . ."

Yes . . . what then?

One could not hang around corridors, hover outside the operating room, or otherwise invite comment on one's curiously unoccupied state.

"I'll go to his office," Honey thought suddenly, "where he has his consultations. And if his secretary is there. . . . Oh, I'll think of *something* to say. To her I shall still be his fiancée." She felt disproportionately cheered at the reflection. "I might even. . . . Well, anyway, I'll see."

Boldness usually pays dividends. And Honey, outwardly calm, however much she might be quaking inwardly, found no difficulty in entering the residence. She gained the safety of her own room without meeting anyone who happened to know that she shouldn't be there.

She changed rapidly, in spite of her trembling fingers that made unusually heavy work of fastening her belt and pinning on her cap. And, thankful that not even Barbara had seen her, Honey went across by the covered way to the hospital building itself with a purposeful but unhurried air.

As she entered the high central hall of Emergency, she experienced terror of what she was doing for a moment. Officially speaking, she had no right to be here at all. She was, according to the records, on leave in London. And it made one feel oddly like a criminal to be putting the official records in the wrong.

However, she went on determinedly. Her expression of thoughtful occupation made her look, she hoped, just like any other busy nurse going about her lawful duties.

Once her heart almost jumped into her throat, because there, only a few turnings ahead of her, was Matron herself. And, incredible though it might seem, Matron always knew where one should be at any given time. Certainly she could not fail to remember that Nurse Milward, who was engaged to Dr. Anston, should be on leave.

But, by great good fortune, Honey reached the elevators just then, and one of them stood open, ready to receive her. The gate clanged behind her. She was whisked upward, away from Matron's dangerously knowledgeable glance and onto the topmost floor, to the surgeons' consulting rooms.

By now Honey's heart was beating heavily, and she found it quite extraordinarily difficult to breathe in anything but shallow little gasps. Just as though she had run up all those flights of stairs instead of taking the elevator.

Outside the last door in the corridor, the door with Dr. Anston's name upon it, she hesitated for almost half a minute. Then she raised her hand and knocked timidly.

A voice immediately bade her, "Come in." But it was not the voice of Dr. Anston. It was the voice of his very competent secretary. And, not knowing whether she was relieved or disappointed by this reprieve, Honey opened the door and entered.

Dr. Anston's secretary was standing before a small mirror, putting on her hat. But she turned at Honey's entrance and said briskly, "Yes, Nurse?"

Then she saw who it was, and her tone changed subtly.

"Oh, Nurse Milward—I didn't realize it was you. I expect you want to see Dr. Anston personally?"

"Yes, please." Honey tried not to sound as frightened as she felt.

"He should be here almost any time now. Do sit down and wait, won't you?"

It was as easy as that!

Honey sat down, nearer the edge of the chair than a self-confident fiancée should have done, and, in an effort to make light conversation, said huskily, "I suppose he's operating?"

"Yes, of course. It was an emergency, and he

expected to be downstairs most of the afternoon."

"I see."

The secretary took a pair of gloves from her top drawer and smoothed them a trifle self-consciously.

"I hope you don't mind if I slip away now. Dr. Anston did say I could go early."

"Why, yes of course." Honey was faintly embarrassed at the implication that explanations were due to her. Almost as though she were more or less the surgeon's wife!

"My boyfriend is home on leave," the other girl explained happily, as she pinned a rose to the lapel of her suit. "He's in the navy, and we hope to be married next year."

"Do you?" said Honey, envying her her simple joys. "How nice."

The secretary laughed slightly at that and glanced curiously at Honey.

"Same pleasant fate for you, isn't it?" she said. "When are you planning your wedding?"

"I—we—haven't decided yet," Honey replied. And then she simply could not add anything else.

So the secretary didn't ask more. But she said goodbye and went away, secretly deciding that Honey was the upstage kind giving herself airs, just because she was engaged to one of the surgeons.

Honey sat on the edge of her chair, clutched her hands tightly together, and wished she had never come.

Why *had* she come, anyway? What was there to say to him, now she was here?

Mechanically she counted her heavy heartbeats and looked around the quiet, somewhat austere office, and thought this is where he interviews people. This is where he talks to them in that quiet, confident reassuring manner. This is where he must have made many decisions that have meant hope and happiness for countless people. Only he can't make any happy or hopeful decision for me.

And then she heard his footstep outside. Before she could even rise to her feet, the door opened and he was in the room.

For a moment he must have mistaken her for his secretary, for that tense, absorbed, exhausted air that followed on any long and anxious operation did not alter. Then suddenly, as though he refocused on a world outside the operating room, he realized who she was and said, "*Honey. . . .*" he stopped a few paces away from her, as though he thought he might frighten her if he came nearer.

"What is it, child?" he asked gently. "How is it you're here and in uniform?"

"I couldn't come any other way." She looked at him with big, frightened eyes, that reflected a good deal of the anxiety she had experienced over her unorthodox behavior.

"I see. And you had to come?" He pulled out the chair behind his desk and dropped into it, a little wearily though his eyes were bright and alert as they observed her. "Why did you have to come, Honey?"

"I thought—" she twisted his ring on her finger, "I—ought to give you back your ring in person, rather than. . . ." She looked down at her hands.

"Oh!" The exclamation was sharp, as though something had annoyed or hurt him. "I meant you to keep that."

"But I couldn't! One never does when . . . when an engagement is broken."

"Not if it's a real engagement, perhaps. But you went through a good deal of unhappiness and embarrassment on my behalf, Honey. I wish you'd keep the ring."

"As a sort of payment, do you mean?" She was horrified.

"No, of course not! Don't be a little idiot."

She was silent, and after a moment he said more quietly, "I'm sorry. I didn't mean to say that. And, in any case, I should have started by apologizing to you."

"For what?" Honey raised her eyes and looked at him.

"For the whole miserable business, I suppose, Honey. But most of all for what happened the other evening."

"The other evening?" She looked puzzled.

"When I kissed you and made you so angry and frightened," he reminded her grimly.

"Oh, that, I wasn't frightened of you," Honey said half to herself.

"You gave a most convincing impression of being so," he told her dryly. "I understood that was why you slapped my face and finally broke the engagement."

"Oh, no." She remembered the slap on his cheek and felt very contrite about it. "It wasn't you that I was frightened of."

"Of whom, then?"

She was silent, suddenly seeing a gulf open at her feet.

"It doesn't matter." She stood up, and with a sudden movement wrenched the ring from her finger and placed it on the desk. "There. There's no point in talking any more about it. I just wanted to return the ring and . . . and go."

"But I don't want you to go, without answering my question." He too stood up, but she slipped past his desk and made for the door.

"Honey. . . ."

But she would not answer the supplication in his tone and grasped the handle of the door.

"Nurse!"

"Sir?" All the discipline of three years' training went into the lightning reaction to that authoritative tone, and she turned immediately. "Come here, please."

"No one wearing the uniform of St. Margaret's could ignore that command, said in that tone. Honey walked back slowly until she stood before him.

"Yes, sir?" she said, with her head bent.

"When I kissed you the other night—" this remark slightly disturbed the nurse-surgeon relationship, but only slightly "—you were desperately frightened about someone or something. You say you were not frightened of me. What were you frightened of then?"

"I don't want to say," Honey told him in a whisper.

"But I insist on knowing." He spoke almost gently that time, but quite determinedly.

Two tears trembled on her gold-tipped lashes. And after a moment he took both her hands in his and said,

"I don't insist on knowing. But won't you tell me?"

"I was frightened," Honey whispered, "because of the way it made me feel. I didn't know by then what was real and what was make-believe. But I wanted . . . I wanted. . . ." She pulled one of her hands away and rubbed it across her eyes like a child.

"What did you want, my darling?" asked Dr. Anston. And, taking her in his arms, he held her so close that Honey felt she and her stiffened uniform went equally limp.

"I wanted it to be true," Honey said with a deep sob and buried her face against him.

"But, my dear, silly little love," said the most distinguished surgeon of St. Margaret's, "It *is* true. Everything that kiss implied is true. I adore you. Don't you know that? You're the most entrancing, fascinating, touching, infuriating and altogether beloved creature to me. Haven't you realized that yet? Didn't you know that I was caught in my own tangle of make-believe almost from the first moment?"

"I couldn't know," exclaimed Honey, her face still hidden against his white coat. "How was I to know? You were talking about perhaps marrying Millicent later, and affecting to cheer me up with the constant reassurance that it would all soon be over?"

"I had to say that, Honey. I didn't know that you'd moved very far from the days when you thought me a monster."

"Oh, you must have known that!" She raised her head and looked at him reproachfully.

"I hoped occasionally and, forgive me now, dearest, I even hoped to make you a little jealous over Millicent. Stupid, I know."

Honey was silent. Then she said slowly,

"It wasn't stupid. I hated her."

Dr. Anston began to laugh at that. And then, as though he recalled that all too recently they had touched tragedy, he stopped laughing and kissed her softly.

"You still haven't told me what all this means, you

know." His eyes were grave, now, and demanding.

"What all . . . what means?"

"Fear of what you felt when I kissed you. Your feeling that you must come and see me. Your jealousy of Millicent. Your letting me hold you in my arms, as I've wanted to for weeks now."

"Oh. . . ." She smiled faintly, and then with a hint of mischief. "I should have thought you could add all that up for yourself without much difficulty."

"But I want you to say it to me, my darling."

His tone was urgent, almost pleading and, looking up at him, she saw for the first time that his usually light gray eyes could look dark with anxiety.

"Oh, darling Dr. Anston—John, I mean. . . ." She flung her arms around him and kissed him, in a way that should have reassured any man. But, just in case he still wanted the whole thing in words, she went on, "I think you're the dearest, most wonderful, fascinating person in the world. And I love you. I'll even take back that bit about your being a monster. Though you are very occasionally if you're angry at anyone," she added, in the interests of strict truth, smiling happily up at him.

He didn't even laugh at that. He returned her kisses with the utmost tenderness, like a man who could not yet quite believe that the sun was shining for him.

"When did you first know?" he asked presently.

"That I loved you?"

"Um-hm."

"I suppose," Honey conceded thoughtfully, "I had the first odd stirring of pride and affection even that afternoon at the Women's Institute meeting."

"Impossible!" he protested with a laugh. "Why then, for heaven's sake? We were on pretty sticky terms then, if I remember rightly." He smiled.

"Yes, I know, but . . . but you spoke so simply and so movingly about your work, and you looked so. . . . Well, I'm not going to tell you all that," she said. "You'll become conceited." But she put up her hand half-timidly against his cheek and smiled at him.

"You don't know what it does to me, to know that you love me and even admire me a little." He smiled down at her, in loving answer. "It doesn't make me conceited—truly, Honey. It just makes me glad to be alive. Come, let me put on your ring again."

And, taking up the ring from the desk where she had put it, he slipped it onto her finger once more.

"This time," he told her firmly, there's no make-believe about it."

"Oh, no, no! It feels," rubbing it gently with her other forefinger, "it feels as though it belongs."

"So it does," he told her. "It was only taken off in mistake. What a good thing," he smiled at her teasingly, "that we hadn't announced our breaking off. At least, not outside the intimate family circle."

"Yes," she agreed. And then. . . . "Oh!" cried Honey, clapping her hand to her mouth, for suddenly she had remembered her woeful conversation with Barbara. She could imagine that devoted friend going around at this very moment, perhaps, tactfully telling everyone that Honey Milward's engagement was off; would they please not say anything about it to her personally?

"May I use your telephone, please? It's frightfully urgent."

She broke away from his tender embrace and had snatched up the receiver even before he could say, "Of course."

Eagerly she demanded to be connected with the nurses' residence. Then she stood there, alternately fuming at the seeming delay and praying that Barbara should, somehow, not yet have begun the tactful and friendly service she had undertaken.

It seemed ages before anyone answered, and then fresh ages before Barbara's voice sleepily said, "Hello."

"Oh, Barbara! It's Honey. Have you told anyone yet about my engagement being broken?"

"No, I have not," replied Barbara crossly over the telephone. "Look, Honey, I've only just woken up. I'd still be asleep, as a matter of fact, if you hadn't called. I haven't had time to get around to—"

"Oh, thank goodness! That's all right. Then don't."

"What did you say?"

"I said, don't. Meaning, don't get around to telling anyone. The engagement isn't broken, after all. In fact, it's all just wonderful. I'll explain later."

There was an eloquent silence. Then Barbara said, "You might give it to me in writing next time, will you? Just to get things straight first time; so you won't have to wake me up when I'm sleeping off night-duty, to tell me you're not engaged and then you are."

"I'm terribly sorry," Honey explained contritely. "But terribly happy too."

"Well, I guess that's all that matters," Barbara said with a laugh. "I don't really mind being woken up to be told that." And then she hung up.

"It's all right." Honey turned a relieved face to Dr. Anston. "She hadn't told anyone."

He looked a good deal amused, but faintly relieved too, Honey thought. For nothing is harder to unsay than good, solid hospital gossip. This was a break!

"Now let's go home and tell Mother." Honey smiled with fresh radiance as she thought how happy her mother would be. "Give me ten minutes to change, and I'll meet you downstairs."

"Make it a quarter of an hour. I have one or two things to attend to here," he replied, with a glance at the pad on his desk. And neither of them noticed that they were talking now like two people who were engaged, and not two people who were pretending to be engaged.

As Honey made her way back to the residence, it was all she could do not to sing or laugh aloud, or otherwise make her rapturous happiness known to all the world. But she contented herself with smiling radiantly at everyone she passed until she suddenly realized that she was beaming at Sister.

She stopped immediately and said, "Why, Nurse—I thought you were on leave." She stared at her.

"Yes, I was—I mean—I am," explained Honey confusedly.

"Then why," enquired Sister, not unreasonably, "are you here, in uniform?"

"Well, I . . . I had to see Dr. Anston. About something very urgent."

"Something private, you mean?"

"Yes. Something private."

"That doesn't quite explain the uniform, does it?" Sister looked piercingly at Honey. "You know as well as I do, Nurse, that you aren't supposed to wear your uniform when you're off duty."

"N-no. But it was the only way of getting into the hospital without comment or question," Honey explained, unable to think of anything but the exact truth, in the emergency of the moment. "And I had to see him."

It is possible that the slight break in Honey's voice conveyed more to Sister than she had intended. At any rate, a slight smile touched her usually severe mouth, and a faintly humorous glint came into her rather fine eyes.

"I see," she said dryly, but not unkindly. "I hope everything is . . . all right now."

"Oh, yes," Honey assured her with candid rapture. "Everything is simply wonderful."

"I'm glad to hear it." Again there was that dry, but rather human note in Sister's voice. "But change into something more suitable for off-duty hours now."

"Yes, Sister. And thank you, Sister, very much," Honey said fervently, before she sped away to her room to change into a dress as Sister suggested.

And, in the glow of happiness that enveloped her at this moment, it seemed to Honey that Sister was an altogether sweet and lovable person.

When she met Dr. Anston a quarter of an hour later, he kissed her as though he had not seen her for a month. And all the way out to Meadlands they talked of how much they loved each other and how silly they had been—which was true, of course—not to have discovered this before.

As they neared home, Honey's eager impatience to tell her mother the good news became almost uncontrollable. When they finally arrived outside the house, she jumped out of the car almost before it had stopped and rushed into the house, crying, "Mother, Mother, where are you?"

But it was her father who came out of the living room, holding his evening paper and demanding,

"What's the matter? Is the place on fire? Why are—"

"Oh, Daddy!" Honey flung her arms around her father. "I'm engaged to John—really engaged, I mean."

Her father kissed her indulgently and said mildly, "Well, that's fine. But I did know that already, you know."

"Oh . . . oh, yes. You did, didn't you?" Shamefaced but radiant, Honey smiled at him, remembering then that he knew nothing of the recent crisis and was therefore hardly in the picture. "I guess I'm a little bit crazy at the moment."

"I guess so," agreed her father kindly. "Most people are when they're engaged. Your mother and I were, as I remember. Hello, John. Come and have a drink."

John Anston paused for a moment to smile at his darling before following Mr. Milward. Perhaps there came to him the sweet, instinctive knowledge that one day, in the far distant future, he would say much the same words to *his* daughter.

Now available!

COLLECTION EDITIONS

of Classic Romances

Harlequin proudly presents a nostalgic collection of the best-selling romance novels of former years. This is a rare series of 100 books, lovingly reissued in beautifully designed new covers. And the cost is only 75¢ each. See complete listing on accompanying pages.

Not sold in stores.

Harlequin Collection Editions

Please note: The number in brackets indicates the original Harlequin Romance number.

Harlequin Collection Editions

*Please note: The number in brackets indicates the
original Harlequin Romance number.*

Harlequin Collection Editions

Please note: The number in brackets indicates the original Harlequin Romance number.

Harlequin Collection Editions

Please note: The number in brackets indicates the original Harlequin Romance number.

Complete and mail this coupon today!

Harlequin Reader Service
MPO Box 707
Niagara Falls, NY 14302

In Canada
Harlequin Reader Service
Stratford, Ontario N5A 6W4

Please send me the following editions of the Harlequin Collection. I am enclosing my check or money order for 75¢ per novel ordered, plus 25¢ to cover postage and handling.

☐ 2	☐ 22	☐ 42	☐ 62	☐ 82
☐ 3	☐ 23	☐ 43	☐ 63	☐ 83
☐ 4	☐ 24	☐ 44	☐ 64	☐ 84
☐ 5	☐ 25	☐ 45	☐ 65	☐ 85
☐ 6	☐ 26	☐ 46	☐ 66	☐ 86
☐ 7	☐ 27	☐ 47	☐ 67	☐ 87
☐ 8	☐ 28	☐ 48	☐ 68	☐ 88
☐ 9	☐ 29	☐ 49	☐ 69	☐ 89
☐ 10	☐ 30	☐ 50	☐ 70	☐ 90
☐ 11	☐ 31	☐ 51	☐ 71	☐ 91
☐ 12	☐ 32	☐ 52	☐ 72	☐ 92
☐ 13	☐ 33	☐ 53	☐ 73	☐ 93
☐ 14	☐ 34	☐ 54	☐ 74	☐ 94
☐ 15	☐ 35	☐ 55	☐ 75	☐ 95
☐ 16	☐ 36	☐ 56	☐ 76	☐ 96
☐ 17	☐ 37	☐ 57	☐ 77	☐ 97
☐ 18	☐ 38	☐ 58	☐ 78	☐ 98
☐ 19	☐ 39	☐ 59	☐ 79	☐ 99
☐ 20	☐ 40	☐ 60	☐ 80	☐ 100
☐ 21	☐ 41	☐ 61	☐ 81	☐ 101

Number of novels checked _____ @ 75¢ each = $_____

Postage and handling $_____.25

                                    TOTAL $_____

NAME _____
(Please print)

ADDRESS _____

CITY _____

STATE/PROV. _____   ZIP/POSTAL CODE _____

Offer expires December 31, 1977

ROM 2061

Send coupon today for
FREE
Harlequin Presents
Catalog

We'll send you by return mail a complete listing
of all the wonderful Harlequin Presents novels
still in stock.

Here's your chance to catch up on all the
delightful reading you may have missed
because the books are no longer available at
your favorite booksellers.

Fill in this handy order form and mail it today.